PIPER DAVENPORT

Quieting the BIKER'S RAGE

DOGS OF FIRE: SAVANNAH CHAPTER BOOK 4

COPYRIGHT

Cover Art
Jackson Jackson

TRIXIE
PUBLISHING

ISBN-13: 9781095382073

ACKNOWLEDGEMENTS

Liz Kelly:
Thanks again. Your insight is always so spot on!

Jack:
Thanks for being my muse, and really great in bed!

PRAISE

All it took was one page and I was immediately hooked on Piper Davenport's writing. Her books contain 100% Alpha and the perfect amount of angst to keep me reading until the wee hours of the morning. I absolutely love each and every one of her fabulous stories. ~ **Anna Brooks – Contemporary Romance Author**

Get ready to fall head over heels! I fell in love with every single page and spent the last few wishing the book would never end! ~ **Harper Sloan, NY Times & USA Today Bestselling Author**

Piper Davenport just reached deep into my heart and gave me every warm and fuzzy possible. ~ **Geri Glenn, Author of the Kings of Korruption MC Series**

This is one series I will most definitely be reading!! Great job Ms. Davenport!! I am in love!! ~ **Tabitha, Amazeballs Book Addicts**

For Sapphire

You inspire me every other week, on Thursdays.
Thanks for that!

Doom

Six Years Ago...

I SMILED AS Aspen Westwood opened the door to her town-house and shook her head. "I told you not to come."

"And I told you I didn't give a shit."

She rolled her eyes, stepping back and waving me inside. She looked adorable in sweats and an oversized T-shirt, her hair pulled up in a messy bun on top of her head. She'd taken her normal brunette hair and gone more of a magenta and she looked cute as hell.

I'd met Aspen a couple of years ago when I'd helped my buddy, Dalton, with a babysitting job. Aspen had been the job, and she and I had hit it off. Well, we'd hit it off as much as gunpowder and matches hit it off. We fucked hard, and fought harder.

"Doom," she said with a sigh. "I need you to hear me. Really hear me."

"I listen better when I'm naked."

She let out a frustrated squeak and dragged her hands down her face.

"Okay, Aspen," I said. "I'm listening."

"This," she waved her hand between us, "is not going to happen."

"It al—"

"Again," she clarified.

"But it's good."

"The sex is, yes, but you're not available."

"Sweetheart, I'm right here."

She gave me a sad smile. "But you're not and you know it. You're angry. Angrier, if that's even possible. I care about you, and I know you care about me, but we don't love each other, and I *know* someone is out there for me, for both of us, who will."

I forced down the rage that threatened to prove her point. "There won't ever—"

"I know." She stroked my face and I reared back like she'd struck me. She dropped her hand and blinked back tears. "Sorry."

"Whatever," I ground out. "I'll leave you alone."

"Stop," she demanded as I turned to leave. "You need to get a handle on this, Doom, or you'll rot from the inside. Talk to someone."

What she didn't understand was that my insides had already festered well past the rot stage and no amount of talking would change that.

"Call me if you wanna fuck, Aspen. See you around."

I walked out her door, climbed on my bike, and rode away.

* * *

Present Day…

I rolled out from under the Lexus I was working on and stood. I'd found the source of the leak and headed toward the parts

2

room just as the sound of screeching tires and crunching metal had me rushing out the front door of the shop.

Alamo and Rabbit were right behind me and we saw a beat up Ford F-150 next to a little Passat in the ditch by the road. The Passat was currently upside down, so we ran for the wreckage.

"Oh my god, that truck rammed into that little car," a woman in a Honda explained as she got out of her car. "He's been following her for several blocks."

"Call 9-1-1," Alamo directed, and he and I focused on the Passat while Rabbit headed to the truck.

I tried to pull the door open, but it wasn't budging. "Ma'am? Can you hear me? What's your name?" She didn't answer right away, so I tried again. "Ma'am?"

"Lyric."

"I'm sorry?"

The woman chuckled. Her sweet laugh gave me pause and I finally looked at her. Jesus, she was gorgeous. Long, blonde hair brushed the roof of her car, giving her almost a halo effect, and when she turned deep blue eyes to me, I nearly lost my breath.

"My name. It's Lyric," she clarified. "My sisters are Harmony and Melody. Mom was obsessed with music and a little bit of a hippie. It's weird, but kind of perfect. Sorry, I'm rambling. Um, can you get me out, please? I feel sick."

"Alamo, she's stuck. Grab a crowbar!" I yelled, then turned back to Lyric. "You hurt?"

"I don't know. All the blood's rushing to my head."

She reached to undo her seatbelt, but I squeezed her hand. "Don't. Let's wait to see what the damage is before we move you."

"Oh," she said. "Right. That's probably a good idea."

I worked to clear the glass covering her, noticing blood on her airbag, so I moved her hair away from her face as gently as I could, parting it at her crown. "You've got a nasty gash on your head."

"What constitutes a nasty one as opposed to a delightful one? Have you ever wondered that?" she asked. "I mean, does the nasty gash call you names instead of bringing you flowers?"

I was pretty sure she was in some sort of pain-induced fugue state, but I couldn't help but notice she was funny as hell.

"What's your name?" she asked.

"Doom."

"Were your parents worried about the end of the world?"

"Something like that," I said, and she smiled. My heart stuttered. Jesus, her smile was stunning.

"Why would they name their baby 'Doom'?" she mused. "You must have been a beautiful baby. That just seems psycho to me." She gasped. "Oh, I'm sorry, I don't mean to call your parents psycho. They're probably very nice people."

"Lincoln Marxx," I said, and then mentally shook myself. I *never* gave anyone my legal name and I couldn't figure out why the fuck I'd blurted it out to this stranger.

"Oh," she rasped. "That's such a cool name. It's kind of a rock star name."

"Crowbar," Alamo said, pulling me out of my head as he shoved the tool into the seam of the doorframe.

"Goddammit," Rabbit bellowed from my right. "Don't move, asshole!"

While Alamo worked on the door, I went to back Rabbit up. He was currently in a fistfight with some redneck who was clearly drunk and I suddenly saw red.

I fuckin' hated drunk drivers.

Rabbit was technically my recruit. I'd met him when he was sixteen right before I'd quit my stint as a firefighter. He'd been a kid on the streets at the time, his parents both dead from ODs and his foster family a shit show who didn't deserve to look after kids. Our club had taken him in and he'd decided to become a prospect when he turned eighteen.

We'd called him Rabbit because he was fuckin' quick in a seriously nervous kind of way. He was a hacking mastermind, too, which helped when we needed information that may or may not be completely legal to obtain.

I rushed for the drunk, grabbing the back of his collar and pulling hard enough to knock him on his ass, where I forced him onto his stomach with a knee in his back. "Where the fuck do you think you're goin'?" I growled.

"Fuck you, asshole," he slurred.

4

"You're not my type." I turned to Rabbit. "Go grab some zip ties."

Rabbit nodded and ran up the embankment back into the shop, returning with two sets of zip ties, which I used to secure the drunk's hands.

Just as I heard sirens in the distance, the drunk made the stupid mistake of trying to wrestle away from me again, so I slammed my fist into his face and he went down hard.

"Watch him," I demanded and made my way back to Lyric.

Alamo had gotten the door open.

"Don't move her!" I called.

"I'm not gonna fuckin' move her, brother," he snapped.

I closed the distance between us and helped Alamo force the door further open.

"I'm going to be sick," Lyric warned and promptly puked everywhere. "Oh my god, I'm so sorry."

"Don't be sorry, sweetheart," Alamo assured. "The EMTs are here. They're gonna take good care of you."

"Y'all are so nice," she mused.

Alamo smiled his million-dollar smile and I found myself scowling in response. It didn't matter that he was married to the woman of his dreams, I didn't want him smiling at Lyric.

"Excuse us," a female voice ordered as she and her partner rolled in a gurney. "Oh, hey, Doom."

"Hey, Marney," I said. She'd been an EMT when I was a firefighter and I liked her. She was crazy as fuck, but fun. "Her name's Lyric. She just threw up, and she's got a laceration on her head."

"Okay, we'll take it from here."

Admittedly, I hovered while they extracted Lyric from her car, and as soon as she was on the gurney, she passed out.

"Fuck," I snapped, stepping toward her.

"We got her," Marney said firmly, placing an oxygen mask over her nose and mouth. "You friends?"

"No," I admitted. "Never met her before."

She raised an eyebrow, but didn't say anything further, and I stepped back to let her work. I watched as they bandaged Lyric's head and loaded her into the ambulance, then I was left to help clean up the scene, since I had a tow truck available for the cops to use.

My shop was right next door to Alamo's. He did mostly mechanical work, I did body work, but we'd cross-pollinate on occasion when we were short-handed or got bored. In the case of the Lexus, he was short-handed, and I had Rabbit training a new guy on paint, so I had a little time on my hands.

Well, until this happened.

I took it upon myself to retrieve anything of Lyric's out of her car that looked valuable and stowed it safely in my saddle-bags until I could get it back to her. I don't know why I did it, but I felt as though it was important.

Once we'd sorted her car, we left the scene for the police to finish up, and I went back to the Lexus I'd been working on. When it was time to close up for the day, I headed back to the compound for a beer...or twelve.

TWO

Lyric

I CAME AWAKE slowly, my face feeling like it had gone a few rounds with Mohammad Ali, and tried to figure out where I was.

"Oh my word, Lyric," Melody cried and sat on the edge of my bed. "You look all swollen and crap."

Classic Melody. Always concerned about how we looked and traveled with her makeup artist, Billy, twenty-four-seven. I was actually surprised he wasn't here with his kit in tow.

"The doctor said you were upside down for a long time."

The memory of the accident flooded back and I grimaced. I still smelled like puke. "Yeah. It wasn't fun."

"You have to have surgery on your leg, huh?"

I nodded. "Apparently so. Tomorrow, I guess."

The doctor had filled me in right before he'd given me some really good drugs that allowed me to sleep for a while.

"Okay, not to make this all about me, but I hope your leg thing isn't contagious."

"I'm sure broken legs don't travel through the air like a virus, DiDi. I mean, you've got a tour coming up. You can't have an injury."

"Exactly. Put that out into the universe," she said. "So, tell me what happened."

I filled her in on everything I remembered, including the two men who helped get me out of my car.

"Miss Morgan?"

Melody stood as a uniformed officer walked into the room.

"Oh, wow, Melody Morgan," the officer said. "I'm a huge fan."

"Really?" Melody breathed out. "That's so sweet."

I rolled my eyes, which severely hurt my head, but I couldn't believe this officer of the law was fangirling over my sister when I was here in a hospital bed.

Melody was the biggest pop star in the world right now, and with three sexy movies under her belt, solidified as one of the most popular actors. All of this adoration for her was par for the course, but I really needed the focus on me right now so we could figure out what happened.

"Ah, sorry, Miss Morgan," the officer said to me. "I'm Officer Jenkins. Do you feel up to a few questions?"

"Sure," I said, and Melody took her seat by the window.

Jenkins pulled out her notebook and gave me a friendly smile which actually put me at ease. "What do you remember?"

"Honestly? I'm not sure what happened. I was at the light and it turned green, when I was suddenly hit from behind, then he came at me from the side and rolled my car."

She nodded. "Okay, that's what the evidence shows as well. The other driver was drunk and he's been taken into custody. We're gathering surveillance footage as we speak."

"What happened to my car?"

"I don't have that information, but I'll see what I can find out for you. I'm pretty sure the insurance company is going to total it."

I sighed. "Poor Petunia."

"Lordy, it's about time you come into this century, LiLi," Melody said with a groan. "You know I'll buy you whatever you want."

And she would, but I could afford my own car, so I glossed over her comment. "Oh, did anyone find my purse at the scene? It didn't make it into the ambulance with me, so I have no ID or anything."

"I'll see what I can find out about that as well." She closed her notebook and smiled again. "Do you have any questions for me?"

My first thought was, *Do you know the name of the man who helped me? Is he single?* But I kept it to myself. "I don't think so."

"Okay. I'll see what I can find out about your personal belongings."

"Thank you."

She wrote down my address and phone number, then left me with my sister again.

"What am I going to do about the charity ball?" I asked, forcing back tears.

Every year my team worked with several of the Savannah fire houses to put on a charity ball to raise money for education on fire prevention, money for families of firefighters who get hurt or die in the line of duty, and general goodwill toward the community. It was my baby and I'd planned the event for the last ten years.

"We've got over a month, sissy," Melody said. "You'll probably be good to go by then."

"I hope so. My case load, though, that's going to be a bit harder."

I was a lawyer and worked for one of the biggest firms in Savannah, along with representing my sister and all the legalities of her career. Melody didn't sign anything until I looked at it. I was right in the middle of a criminal trial, defending a man I knew was innocent, which was the worst client to have. It would be a hell of a lot easier to represent him if he was guilty.

Unfortunately, I'd have to hand him off to my second chair, Georgia Slidell, but this would give her the chance to rise to the occasion.

"You'll figure it out," Melody encouraged. "And I can help with the benefit. I'm home for two months."

"You have to get ready for your tour."

She shrugged. "It'll all work out. You'll see."

"I hope so."

I was exhausted, so Melody hung out in my room while I dozed, trying to put aside my worries, at least for a little while.

* * *

Doom

"What's all that?" Alamo asked, nodding toward the small box on the club dining room table.

Alamo was the Sgt. At Arms for the Savannah Chapter of the Dogs of Fire MC, and I was technically under him as Road Captain.

"All the shit from Lyric's car," I said.

Alamo twisted off the top of a beer, handing it to me before taking a swig of his own. "Lyric?"

"The woman who got hit yesterday."

"Why do you have it?"

I shrugged. "Just didn't want her stuff to walk away with some asshole."

"You gonna get it back to her?"

"Was thinkin' about it."

Alamo raised an eyebrow, but didn't respond.

"What?" I challenged.

He smiled, taking another swig of beer and swallowing. "What, what?"

"Fuck you."

Alamo chuckled and walked away. Jesus, he was a dick. I pulled my phone out of my pocket and called Marney.

"Hey, Doom. You okay?"

"Yeah," I said. "Just checkin' on the woman you guys took in yesterday."

"I can't give you any information, buddy."

"I just need to get her shit back to her. Is she still in the hospital?"

"I think that's a good assumption."

"Thanks, I appreciate it."

"No problem. Are you coming out for the charity dinner?"

The local emergency services departments put on a ball every year and the Dogs served as security for the event. This year was a little different for me, because I'd be doing double-duty as a pawn in their live auction, "Win a Date With a Firefighter." How the fuck I got roped into that, I don't know.

Oh, yeah I did, Alamo signed me and Rabbit up. I needed to remember to put laxative in his coffee.

"Yeah, I'll be there," I promised.

"See you then."

I hung up and loaded the boxed items into my saddlebags, before heading to the hospital. I hoped they didn't give me a hard time about seeing her. I was admittedly in the mood for a fight and pretty much anyone would do.

* * *

Lyric

I awoke to an empty room, and in unbearable pain. I couldn't stop a whimper as I shifted in the bed to find the call button for the nurse.

"Shit," a deep voice hissed. "You okay?"

My gaze flew toward the sound and I gasped. "You."

"Yeah, me," he said, his eyebrows furrowed in concern. "You need a nurse?"

"Yes," I cried out as I sat up and my leg protested the movement.

He rushed into the hallway and yelled for a nurse, and one came rushing in within seconds.

"She's in pain," Lincoln explained.

The nurse checked my chart, then shot something into my IV and I was no longer in pain. "Thank you," I rasped, smacking my lips together.

"I'm Shauna and I'll be here with you until the morning. You can't eat or drink anything, but I can get you some ice chips to help with the dry mouth."

I nodded and Shauna left me with the ridiculously hot stranger. "What are you doing here?" I asked, but I'm pretty sure it came out as, "What kdjkdkdjkdjjfjk, phhht?"

He smiled. "I brought everything I could rescue from your car."

"You did?"

"Yeah." He nodded toward the window. "It's all there. Your purse and laptop, along with some notebooks."

"Thank you," I whispered. "Those were all of my case notes. I'd have been screwed without those."

"Case notes?"

"I'm a lawyer," I explained. I think. I had no idea exactly how it was coming out of my mouth.

"You don't take notes on your computer?"

I shook my head. "I remember better when I write them down. Plus, no one can hack the information."

He smiled.

Lordy, he's a beautiful man.

His eyes crinkled deeper and he chuckled. "Thank you."

"Oh my god, did I just say that out loud?"

"You absolutely did."

I blushed squeezing my eyes shut tight. "It's the drugs."

"No doubt."

I heard the squeak of leather and opened my eyes again. "Are you leaving?"

"Yeah. You take care."

He suddenly sounded angry. "Okay. Um, thanks for saving my life...and my stuff."

"Yeah, no problem. See you around."

"Wait!" I called, I have no idea why, but he turned to face me slowly. "Thank you, Lincoln. Truly. What you did was incredibly kind and I appreciate it. If you ever need anything, please don't hesitate to call me, okay?"

He nodded, the cloud surrounding him growing darker, then he was gone and I was left surprisingly bereft and confused by his departure, but was so tired, I fell asleep before I could unpack those emotions.

* * *

Doom

What the fuck did I just do?

I headed back to my bike and paced for a few minutes in an effort to calm down. Jesus, she'd called me Lincoln. No one had called me Lincoln in ten years.

Goddammit!

I needed to figure out a way to stay far far away from this woman.

Climbing on my bike, I got the fuck outta Dodge and headed back to the club. Walking in, I found our president, Doc, in an epic, knock-down-drag-out with his woman, Olivia. This wasn't new. All they did was fight. Well, all they did in public was fight. But tonight was something a little different. Tonight, Olivia was crying. This was not normal. Or right.

"What the fuck, Doc?" I demanded.

I usually didn't get involved in things of a personal nature, but when a woman I cared about was crying, I tended to investigate.

"It's not him, Doom," Olivia rushed to say. "It's been a shitty day and I took it out on Tris." Doc threw his hands in the air and walked away, and Olivia cried harder. "Tristan!" she called.

"At some point, Liv, you're gonna have to pull your head out of your ass."

"Fuck you, Doom."

I crossed my arms and leaned toward her. "You offerin'?"

She let out a snort of derision. "You wish."

"You might wanna go deal with that," I said, and gave a chin lift in the direction Doc headed.

She rolled her eyes, but finally made her way toward Doc's room.

I headed to the kitchen for a bottle of beer.

Lyric

Three weeks later…

 T SUCKED. CRUTCHES sucked. Everything sucked and I wanted out of my damn house. Melody had gone back to her twelve hour rehearsals, so I had no one to talk to but my cat, Booger. And Booger was an asshole.

"Meow."

I glanced down at Booger sitting at my feet, his tail flicking back and forth and asked, "What?"

"Meow."

"In case you haven't noticed, *sir*, I'm unable to cater to you

14

right now."

"Meow."

"Booger, seriously."

He stood, turning his butt to face me and looking at me because I just *knew* he was plotting my death, then with another swish of his tail, he walked away.

"You really are a dick," I muttered. "Even though you're showing me respect right now. I'm not impressed," I called.

"Meow."

"Always have to have the last word, don't you?" I complained, then groaned. "I'm sitting here talking to my cat. Jebus, I have officially become a cat lady."

My phone buzzed and I snagged it off the side table. "Hello?"

"Hey, LiLi," Harmony said, and I let out a sigh of relief.

"Hi, NiNi. How are you?"

Harmony was the sister between me and Melody and she was absolutely my best friend. She was currently living in Portland, Oregon with her FBI husband and two kids, Skyler and Ares, and was happy, which was all I'd ever wanted for her.

"Well, I'm driving up to the house. Are you okay with me parking in the garage?"

My heart raced with glee. "What?"

She chuckled. "You heard me. Process faster, LiLi, I'm almost home."

"Yes, you can park in the garage," I rushed to say, even though I was too nervous to believe she was actually here.

"Okay, I've got my app on my phone, so don't you dare get up. I'll be in in a minute."

Less than five minutes later, my sister walked in and I burst into tears.

Harmony dropped her purse on the floor and rushed to me, kneeling in front of the recliner I'd been stuck in. "Oh, honey, is it that bad?"

"I'm an introvert, god damn it! I should be okay being alone, but I'm so incredibly bored, I've started having conversations with Booger. And they're *deep*, NiNi. Solve the problems of the world deep."

Harmony bit back a laugh, her eyes dancing with mirth. "Well, I'm here, so we can let Booger go back to being a dick and *I'll* help you fix the world."

I nodded and smiled through my tears. "How long do I get you?"

"One week. Jaxon and I just closed a huge case, so I got a week's reprieve."

"And you came *here*?"

"Yeah, sissy, I came here. Jaxon's coming in a couple of days if that's okay with you. We left the kids with Aidan and Kim, although Cassidy has threatened to steal them, so they're going to be spoiled while I boink my man hard and often. I hope that's okay."

"That means you'll be here for the benefit," I whispered, ignoring the boinking information.

Harmony grinned. "Yep. We sure will. I can help with any last minute logistics and Jax will be here for heavy lifting."

I burst into more sobbing again and Harmony hugged me. "I got you, sissy. Everything's going to be okay. I'm going to get the rest of my stuff, okay? You good for the moment?"

"Yes," I said with a sniff, and smiled again. Harmony headed out of the room and I let out a deep sigh of relief.

Once she settled her stuff upstairs, Harmony forced me out of my chair and made me move a little, then we turned on some old Journey on vinyl and sat down to finalize the plans for the best charity dinner ever.

By the time Melody got home from rehearsals, I was feeling a lot more human, especially after Harmony cooked. My sister and I both enjoyed cooking but Harmony *loved* it with her whole being and her creations showed that.

* * *

Saturday morning arrived, and I'd barely slept the night before. As much as we'd managed to accomplish this past week, we still had a shit ton to do and I was using a walker or forced to be in a chair, unable to move freely on my own.

Thank God for Harmony. And Melody as well, really. She'd figured out a way to get a night off so that she could do a private concert, which meant we sold twice the amount of tickets than last year. Plus, according to Wynn, who was handling both the silent and live auctions, she had some amazing donations, not to mention gorgeous men, to auction off.

Jaxon had arrived on Wednesday and rallied a few of his FBI buddies to help with some heavy lifting, which was more valuable than he could know, and I probably thanked him twelve times a day.

I was currently sitting at my dining room table, going through my final checklist when Harmony walked in. "Are you ready to head over to the Convention Center?"

"Yes, give me five," I said, distractedly.

She chuckled. "You said that half-an-hour ago."

"Did I?"

I was forced to move my hands away from my keyboard when Harmony closed my laptop on me. "Yes. We have everything in the car. Let's go."

"Okay, okay, I'm coming." I grabbed my crutches and hoisted myself up, following her slowly out to the car. I was in a T-shirt, shorts, and flip flops, which Harmony had objected to, but I just couldn't shove my good foot into a sneaker. It was too hot. And there was no way I was going to put my formal gown on until the very last minute. I just had to be extra careful and make sure I didn't trip on anything.

Jaxon met me at the top of my porch stairs, took my crutches from me, and lifted me down before handing me back my crutches. God, he was a good guy. Gentleman to the nth degree and I was so glad my sister and he had found each other.

He helped me into the back seat of his rental and then we headed down to the convention center where we'd be watching Melody rehearse and take care of any last minute details.

We parked close to the side entrance and I hobbled inside and bumped into something hard. I looked up to find my savior standing with a group of rough looking bikers and I let out a quiet gasp. "What are you doing here?"

Lincoln frowned. "Should you be on your feet?"

"I need to be up and moving a few hours a day," I said.

Oh my god, he looked incredible. Last time I saw him, he

wore torn jeans, a leather jacket, motorcycle boots, and a beanie covering every inch of his head. I had no idea if he had hair or what color it was.

The man had hair. A lot of it. It was dark. It was long… shoulder-length…and thick with a slight curl. It gave him a Jason Momoa look, if Jason Momoa was an angry motorcycle type. It complemented his full beard perfectly and made my girly bits long for things it shouldn't. Shit, he was gorgeous.

"Maybe you should sit down," he said.

"I'm good," I said, surprised by his demand. "Why are you here?"

He rolled his eyes.

"He's one of the auction items," his friend answered. "You're Lyric, right?"

"Ah, yes."

"I'm Alamo. You crashed in front of my shop."

"Oh," I breathed out. "Thank you so much for all your help."

"Did you get another car sorted?"

I shook my head. "I figured I'd wait until I could actually drive again."

"Good plan," he said, and nodded toward Lincoln. "You need help findin' another one, Doom's your man."

Lincoln shook his head and glared at his friend. "Alamo," he growled.

I smiled, feeling incredibly insecure all of a sudden. "I'm sure I'll be fine on my own."

"Alamo?" Jaxon walked in with a huge grin on his face.

"What the fuck are you doin' here, Jax?" he asked, giving him a brotherly greeting.

"Helping Lyric out with the event. What are you doing here?"

"Doom and Rabbit are getting auctioned off, and there was no way in hell I was gonna miss that."

"You know each other?" I asked.

"Aidan and Carter are members of their MC in Portland. I met Alamo a couple of years ago when I was helping out on a case." Jaxon turned and reached his hand out as Harmony walked over to us. "This is my wife, Harmony."

"No shit?" Alamo said. "You two sisters?"

"Guilty," I said, and stole a glance at Doom who was watching me closely with a scowl on his face. Weird.

"Melody's the third sister," Jaxon said, almost in warning.

"Melody Morgan?"

"Yes," I said. "We should probably get to work."

"Lyric Morgan?"

I lifted my head to see Quinlan Westgate walking toward me. Actually, I wasn't sure if she was still Westgate, as I'd heard through the Savannah gossip line that she'd gotten a divorce. "Quin? Hi!"

"What the heck happened to you?"

"Drunk driver," I said.

"Holy crap. That looks painful."

"Yeah, it kind of is. More a pain in the butt," I admitted. "I don't have time for this, you know?"

She smiled gently. "I get it."

"Did you get roped into volunteering?"

Quinlan had been part of Savannah Society for as long as I'd known her, and we'd met at a charity event almost ten years ago. She was always helping someone with something. She was one of the sweetest people I'd ever met.

"I'm here with my husband, actually."

"Wait." I tried to keep the disgust of my face. "Didn't you and Michael get divorced?"

"Oh, we did. I'm remarried. To Knox." She gave a chin lift to the group of bikers. "He's the drop dead gorgeous blond man watching me like a hawk."

I chuckled. "Well done."

She grinned. "Thank you. We're here for moral support for Doom, but seriously, if you need anything, please let me know. Jasmine's on her way as well. She's married to Alamo."

I nodded. "Thank you. I'll definitely let you know. We'll be inside watching Melody until I can't take it anymore."

"You don't live to watch your sister gyrate on stage?"

"Can't say that I do, no."

Quin laughed. "Hey, let's get together for dinner sometime. Better yet, I'll let you know when we're doing a girls' night."

"That sounds fun," I said. "Thanks."

"I'll text you." She hugged me, then made her way back to her husband. Doom was still watching me, his face scowling, and I couldn't for the life of me understand what I'd done to offend him.

Harmony and Jaxon were still chatting with the group, so I continued on, my leg on fire with every step, but I really didn't want to take anything that would cloud my mind. I needed to be alert and on top of everything tonight.

I stopped my hobbling and took a few deep breaths.

"You in pain?"

I jumped, seriously jostling my tentative hold on gravity, and found strong arms wrapping around my waist to steady me.

"You need to get off your feet," Lincoln growled.

I tried to push him away, but he didn't budge. "I'm fine."

"Baby, your face shows everything and you look like you're in a shit ton of pain."

I tried to stand taller, hard to do when being held tightly by a demigod and using crutches to stay upright. "First, I'd appreciate it if you didn't call me baby. Second, whether or not I'm in pain is really none of your concern. Now, if you'd please release me, I have work to do."

"Jesus," he whispered.

"Jesus doesn't really factor into this," I sassed. "I'm the one who's going to have to navigate the auditorium steps."

"Lyric!" my sister called. I craned my neck and she frowned. "You okay?"

"You're asking me *now*?" I retorted. "After I nearly fell flat on my face?"

"You were never gonna fall," Lincoln countered. "I had you."

I raised an eyebrow. "You also do not factor into this, Lincoln."

"She's good," Lincoln called out. "I'll help her inside."

"No you won't."

"Yeah, I will."

"Jesus," I hissed.

He smirked. "Jesus doesn't factor into this."

I rolled my eyes as he turned my words back on me.

"Ready?" he asked.

"I can—"

"Need you to let me help you, Lyric, 'cause if you end up flat on your gorgeous ass, I'm gonna have a problem with that."

"You think my ass is gorgeous?" I asked, then immediately added, "Don't answer that."

He scowled again. "I think everything about you is gorgeous."

"Stop," I hissed. "Just help me inside and leave me be."

"Your wish is my command."

He took one of my crutches, wrapped his arm around my waist and helped me down the shallow auditorium steps.

"What the fuck is that?" he grumbled.

"Melody's rehearsing," I answered.

Melody stopped dancing and frowned. "Are you okay?"

I nodded, but I could tell she didn't believe me.

"Let's take five," Melody said, and jumped off the stage, rushing over to me. "You look really pale, LiLi."

"I'm fine," I lied.

"Who are you?" Melody asked.

"Doom."

"What kind of a name is Doom?" Melody demanded.

"It's his club name," I provided. "You can let me go now, Lincoln."

He settled me in one of the chairs and stood, crossing his arms. "How long ago did you take a pain pill?"

I checked my wrist which was void of a watch. "Oh, about five o'none of your business."

"Did you take one at four?" Melody asked.

"No," I said.

"Why not?"

Again, this came from my sister.

I sighed. "Because I need to be able to think tonight."

"You won't if you're in pain."

This came from Doom.

"Yeah, what he said," Melody retorted.

"Both of you need to walk away right now."

"And if we don't?" Doom challenged.

I forced back frustrated tears as I took several deep breaths. I needed everyone to stop fussing over me. I hated fussing. It put me on edge.

"Oh, shit, my sister is going to cry," Melody informed Doom. "And if Lyric cries, the world ends, so I'm going to find Harmony and get her some pain meds that she is going to take, even if I have to force them down her fucking gullet."

She stalked away and Doom hunkered down in front of me. "You gonna cry, Angel?"

I glared at him. I couldn't handle him giving me a sweet nickname while he was standing in front of me looking positively edible, because he was right, I did want to cry and that wasn't in my M.O. "I don't cry."

As if to prove I was lying, he swiped his thumb over my cheek and gently wiped a tear away. His touch scorched me and I leaned back. "Don't."

He slid his thumb into his mouth and sucked on it, staring at me as he did it, and my girly bits contracted with need. I was pretty sure he knew exactly what he was doing to my body and I had to look away.

I hadn't had sex in close to three years and my body was suddenly in dire need.

"What's this about not taking your meds at four?" Harmony demanded as she arrived with Melody in tow.

"I need to be on point, NiNi. I can't be foggy."

She handed me a bottled water and a pill and leaned down. "Take it."

"Ni—"

"Take the damn pill, LiLi."

"First, I'm not an errant child—"

"If you don't take the pill voluntarily, Lyric, I'm gonna make it my mission to make you," Doom warned.

I took the pill.

It wasn't lost on me that my sisters couldn't stop looking between me and Doom, a bit like they were watching a tennis match, and I decided I'd had enough. "I'd appreciate it if y'all would fuck off now, so I can get some work done."

"Jaxon's carrying everything into the dressing room, so I'll go grab your laptop," Harmony offered.

"Thanks," I said, and my sisters went their separate way.

Doom, however, lingered.

"You can go too," I said.

He leaned down. "Open."

"Open what?"

"Your mouth." He crossed his arms. "For now."

I shivered even as I wrinkled my nose. "I will not."

"Did you cheek your meds?"

"What?" I snapped. "No."

"Open so I can see."

"Oh my god, Lincoln—"

He leaned in, almost nose-to-nose with me and whispered a sexy threat, "If you don't want me to kiss you, and investigate personally if that pill went down your throat, you better open your goddamn mouth."

Call me crazy, but I suddenly wanted him to kiss me.

Instead, I opened my mouth and raised my tongue.

Doom looked as disappointed as I felt as he stood again.

"Doom!"

We both looked to see a woman waving him over. I didn't recognize her, but I deduced it was one of Wynn's assistants. Wynn was organizing the auction and I know she'd asked several firefighters to help her with it.

"Fuck," he breathed out. "You good?"

I took a deep breath. "As I've said, *multiple* times, I'm fine."

"Well, yeah, damn fine, but are you okay?"

"Doom!" she called again.

"Goddammit."

I cocked my head. "You better go."

He nodded and walked away just as Harmony returned with my computer. "Who is that?"

"He was the man who rescued all my stuff from my car after the accident."

"He seems to like you."

"No he doesn't," I ground out. "He's kind of rude."

Actually, demanding was more accurate, but that made me like him a little, and I didn't want to like him at all.

"Oh my god, LiLi, that dude is into you," Melody breathed out, flopping into a chair next to me.

"Don't you have work to do?"

"Yep. But not for ninety seconds." She faced me. "Now, tell me about the hottie."

"There's nothing to tell," I said, opening my laptop.

"Oh, there's something to tell," Harmony countered, taking the seat on the other side of me. "Spill."

"We have so much to do. Can we please shelve this?" I begged.

"No," Melody said.

"*Yes*," Harmony countered, with an emphasis on the 's.'

"Killjoy," Melody grumbled, and headed back to the stage, while Harmony leaned down and kissed my cheek.

"You have a reprieve until tonight."

"Whatever," I retorted, and went back to my list.

Harmony chuckled and walked away.

FOUR

Lyric

"**Y**OU LOOK GORGEOUS," Harmony crooned as I shuffled out of the dressing room.

I smiled. Melody's make-up artist and stylist had worked wonders, weaving my long blonde hair into an intricate braided bun on the side of my neck, leaving a few wisps of hair to fall around my face. My makeup was light, but he'd done a daring smoky eye, a light blush and a nude lip which complemented my Zac Posen gown perfectly.

The sleeveless, deep blue gown, had a plunging v-neckline, and the front was knotted, which hid my small pooch (I loved milk duds, sue me). It had a mermaid silhouette, but the tulle skirt was flared, so my leg brace was hidden. I wore one of my Loubouton peep toed heels, but I was regretting this choice slightly, because my crutches had been measured based on my natural height, not with a four-inch heel on.

But they were Loubouton. Fuck my crutches.

I followed my sisters to our table and saw that Wesley O'Neal and his CFO, Charles Alder, were already seated and I smiled. "This is not your table, sir."

Wesley and I had been friends for a few years. He owned quite a bit of Savannah real estate and beyond, and I'd represented his firm when a rival company had wanted to buy one of his properties. The problem was, they wanted to do it illegally, so they paid a low-level guy in the city building inspector's office to plant evidence that Wes had been less than honest in how he'd procured the building originally.

The thing about Wes was, he was honest to a fault. Not a pushover, mind you, but always told the truth and his handshake was his bond, real old-school stuff. It took over a month to find the evidence, but we did, and it had solidified our friendship outside of a professional relationship.

He grinned wide, standing and making his way to me before leaning down to kiss my cheek. "I know, but I was stuck with Gordon Snyder and I just could not sit there all night and listen to the wonders of six hundred CCs versus two hundred CCs. So, I secretly switched tags with Marvin Aikers."

I grimaced. "Well, I'd like to know who the hell Marvin Aikers thinks he is, because he wasn't originally sitting at my table. Sneaky little bastard."

"You're welcome."

I laughed. "My hero."

"Come, sit," he ordered and nodded to my injury. "Tell me how this happened. I'm assuming it was while you were doing some kind of ninja move on a perp."

"I'm a lawyer, Wes, not a cop." I chuckled and nodded to Harmony. "That's NiNi's thing. She's FBI. Oh, by the way. Harmony, meet Wes. Wes, my sister Harmony and her husband Jaxon. You probably already know Melody."

We spent a few minutes greeting each other, then a server arrived to take our order and open bottles of wine and take alternate drink orders.

Before I knew it, dinner was over and it was time for me to

do my 'thing.'

"You're up," Harmony said, waving to the podium and I nodded, heading to the stairs at the side of the stage.

Wes helped me up them, then I made my way to the middle of the stage and leaned against the podium. The room was packed, every table bought and filled, and the cash bar already running out of red wine. Jaxon had taken a couple of Doom's brethren on a wine run, once again saving the night.

"Hello everyone," I said, glad I'd been forced to take a pain pill earlier. There was no way I would've been able to stand there without it. "Thank you so much for coming tonight. I look forward to all of you giving generously in our various auctions. I have it on good authority the firefighters who have graciously donated their time are going to be well worth your donations. Even I have been kept in the dark, so I'm just as excited as you are."

* * *

Doom

"I want to take a moment to thank…"

I tuned out Lyric's obligatory thank you speech as I stood back stage and waited for my personal hell to begin. Jesus, I should have just murdered Alamo, hid his body, then pretended I never got signed up for this shit.

Part of my hell came in the form of Lyric Morgan and the gown that begged to be slowly removed from her body. I'd spent most of the evening forcing my dick to behave every time I caught a glimpse of her legs (boot and all) in the short shorts she'd been wearing earlier, and now her evening gown. Jesus, she was stunning.

"I really hope some old lady doesn't bid on me," Rabbit lamented.

I rolled my eyes. "I'm hopin' no one bids on me, period."

He grinned. "Have you seen the sheer number of high-class pussy out there? I'm good with anyone under the age of forty-five."

"That's because you're young, dumb, and full of cum."

Rabbit bobbed his head up and down. "Hell, yeah, I am."

"Jesus," I hissed as I closed my eyes and shook my head.

"I'm going to turn the evening over to Wynn Porter, she'll be introducing your auction items! Please give her a warm welcome."

The place erupted with applause and Wynn took her place on the stage. Wynn was gorgeous. She was probably in her mid-thirties and spoke softly, but confidently. She'd always been cool to me, and even though I hadn't known her very long, I got a good feeling from her.

Rabbit got called up and I watched as he jogged onto the stage like a fuckin' Labrador puppy, all legs and stupidity. In the end, some woman, well over forty, bid five-grand on the boy, and Wynn hit the gavel down and it was done.

To Rabbit's credit, he covered his disappointment like a champ and headed off the stage the opposite way, right as Wynn caught my eye. She smiled slowly and I shook my head.

Well, shit.

"Ladies, we have a real treat for you tonight."

I tried to keep a scowl off my face as I made my way out of the dark.

"This man was a firefighter with the Savannah Fire Department for ten years before leaving to open his own body shop. So, ladies, he both knows how to use his hose, and pound out your dents."

I bit back a groan as the laughter filled the room.

"And don't let his name fool you," she said, waving me onto the stage, "because his name might be Doom, but he'll make your heart go zoom."

I heard a gasp to my left and followed the sound to find Lyric standing on her crutches, her mouth open in shock. I forced myself not to smile as Wynn continued to make really bad puns at my expense.

"Four-thousand," a woman yelled, standing in the back and waving her arms.

"Four-thousand, five-hundred," another one yelled.

"Five-thousand."

Wynn looked like she might squeal with glee as the number

kept going up and up.

"Twelve-thousand dollars!"

A collective gasp sounded, and everyone turned to try and find the generous benefactor.

Shit. It was Melody Morgan.

"Thirteen thousand."

My head whipped to the woman who'd originally bid four, and my stomach churned. Option one was a certifiably crazy woman and option two was a woman who'd had more dent repair than Lyric's car.

"Fifteen thousand," Melody countered.

"Sixteen thousand."

And so it went until Melody bid fifty-thousand and the other woman finally accepted defeat.

"Well," Wynn crooned, fanning herself with her auction program. "I'm not sure how we're going to top that. Melody Morgan, you've won a date with Firefighter Doom."

I stalked off the stage as soon as I could, nearly ramming into Lyric. I reached out to steady her as I passed her. "Sorry."

* * *

Lyric

"No, I'm sorry," I rushed to say. "I was kind of blocking the exit."

I couldn't stop staring at Doom as he headed off the stage like his feet were on fire. Probably eager to get his date with my sister started.

"You feelin' okay?" he asked.

"Yep. Fantastic."

He studied me like he was staring into my soul and I dropped my gaze, unable to hold his. "You sure you're okay?"

"Um, yes, I'm great. I should really get back to it."

"Okay, Angel, you get back to it."

He still held me steady and I turned in order to break his hold. He held tight.

"LiLi, you need to get off your feet," Harmony demanded walking toward me. "Honey, your job is over, you can relax."

"You're probably right," I conceded, giving Doom a chin lift in challenge.

"You have a good rest of your night," he said, finally releasing me and walking away.

"What was that all about?" Harmony asked.

"I have no idea."

"Why did Melody bid fifty-thousand dollars on him?" Harmony asked. "Did you give her permission to do that?"

"Outside of the fact, this is technically charitable giving, she hasn't spent all of her 'fun' money this month," I said with a sigh. "Believe it or not, she stayed under the limit. She still has a thousand to do with as she pleases."

I'd always had Melody on a budget, but I'd had to tighten the purse strings so to speak when her first, then third husband had tried to take her for more than the prenup. Neither of them banked on me, and they found out what hell felt like when they messed with the Morgan sisters. Husband number two scurried away like the rat he was, but I never knew where husband number four might be lurking, so I'd clamped down the flow of cash.

Jebus, maybe Doom was husband number four.

"She's spent almost a hundred thousand already?" Harmony asked.

"Yep. She bought llamas."

"Llamas?"

"And alpacas."

"Jebus," Harmony hissed. "What the hell does she need llamas and alpacas for?"

"No clue," I said.

"Well, I'm glad I don't have to care anymore."

Harmony had been Melody's assistant for years. Right up until she met Jaxon, actually. Melody had gotten out of control and since I wasn't on the road with them, Harmony took the brunt of all of that. Melody had gone through six assistants since Harmony quit, but so far, her most recent one, Brandy, seemed to be sticking. She'd been hired two years ago and was still here.

"Lucky you," I deadpanned, and Harmony smiled.

"This guy seems to like you."

"No he doesn't," I ground out.

"Okay." Harmony shrugged. "He doesn't. How did you meet?"

"He's the one who rescued all my belongings from my car after the crash."

"Oh, right," she said. "I heard about that. Didn't he also beat the shit out of the guy who hit you?"

"Did he?"

"Apparently so," Harmony confirmed.

"How do you know that?"

"I have my ways," she said.

"What ways?"

"Just ways."

"NiNi."

"Jaxon found out everything when he did a deep dive into the crash."

"Why is Jaxon doing a deep dive into the crash?" I snapped.

"Because I asked him to."

I took a deep breath and dropped my head so I didn't squeal like a banshee. "Harmony, sweetness, why did you ask him to look into the crash?"

"Because he has contacts here that I don't."

"I swear to God, sissy, I'm about to lose my religion," I ground out.

"Sorry." Harmony sighed. "I know I'm being purposely obtuse, but I didn't really want to talk about this here. Can we talk when we get home? I promise I'll tell you everything."

"Fine," I said. I was too tired to think right now anyway, and I didn't have the energy to fight with her.

"I'm going to grab our stuff and we'll get out of here, okay?" Harmony said. "Jaxon's going to stay behind and help clean up."

"He doesn't need to do that, NiNi, the event center will take care of it."

"But he will make sure all of your stuff makes it home safely."

"Okay. Thank you," I said, and Harmony left me.

"Sit," Doom demanded, appearing behind me with a folding chair.

"Where did you come from?"

"Just behind the stage. Take a seat, Angel."

"Doom, I—"

"Just sit in the goddamn chair, Lyric," he said as he unfolded it.

I lowered myself into it, nearly crying out in relief.

He hunkered in front of me and removed my heel, giving my foot a squeeze, then standing again. "You should take something."

"I'm okay."

"Or you could stop being brave when you don't have to be and take a pain pill."

I cocked my head and studied him for several seconds. "What is your deal?"

"What do you mean?"

I shook a finger at him. "You want people to think you're an asshole, but you're not."

He let out a hiss which meant I'd hit pay dirt.

"You good?" he snapped.

"I'm great," I snapped back.

He turned on his heel and stalked away and I couldn't help a smile. I was beginning to put the pieces of one Lincoln 'Doom' Marxx together and I was liking what I saw.

"You look like the canary who swallowed the cat," Harmony mused as she walked toward me.

I shook my head. "I think I'm just tired and losing my mind."

"Well, let's get you home and tucked into bed. You deserve to sleep for a couple of days."

"That sounds amazing."

* * *

Doom

I climbed on my bike and headed to Burt's, an underground fight club that changed locations every month or so. I didn't always go...but I always knew where it was, just in case I needed to get out some frustration.

Which I did.

Right fucking now.

I pulled up and headed inside, the smell of blood and sweat strangely calming to me. My heart raced a little as I pushed through the crowd and stood at the edge of the circle.

"You come for a fight?"

The question came from my left and I looked that way to find Burt sidling up to me. He had a half-smoked, fatty cigar clenched in his teeth and his shirt was unbuttoned enough to see more hair than a seventies porn star, complete with gold chains gleaming in the low light.

"Yeah," I said.

"On a scale of one to ten?"

"Twelve."

"Shit," he said, but he grinned. There was nothing Burt loved more than money, well, except blood, so the fact he knew I was itchin' for a fight meant he had someone who could draw enough to make me hurt.

"You got someone good?" I asked.

"I got someone mean."

I grinned. "Perfect."

"Iggy'll be your second."

"Whatever," I replied. I didn't really care who watched my back. I wanted to hurt. I needed pain to wash away the beauty I'd experienced tonight. I didn't deserve it and I needed a re-minder of that fact.

"I'll be back in a few."

I gave him a chin lift and focused back on the current fight. The knockout didn't take long and the crowd was a little disap-pointed that the carnage was quick, but this just gave Burt an opportunity to rile them up again with what he had in store.

"We got a special treat for you assholes!" he called over the mic, nodding toward me. "This here's Doom. He's in the mood for a challenge, so I'm gonna give him one."

The crowd's din grew and Burt turned waving his arm. A gi-ant of a man emerged from the back and I couldn't stop a smile. Yes. This was exactly what I wanted.

At six-foot-four, I was not small, but the man I was going to fight dwarfed me and I knew I was going to enjoy this battle.

I walked into the circle, removing my cut and T-shirt as I went, handing everything off to Iggy, then meeting my opponent in the middle. Burt walked the perimeter, taking bets, then met us in the middle with a huge smile. "You know the rules."

We both nodded and Burt walked into the crowd.

The hit that came, came hard and I relished it. But I didn't let it happen again. Because my opponent was several inches taller than me, I focused on his kidneys and got several jabs in. We sparred for three minutes before the bell rang then we rested for a minute. Iggy gave me water and patched me up as best he could, then we were back in.

I don't remember anything after that, just the blessed black that covered me as unconsciousness came.

* * *

"Jesus Christ, Doom," Doc hissed, pushing away from his truck.

"Whad-dar-you-doin-here?" I slurred through my swollen, bloody mouth.

"Burt called."

Iggy handed me off to him and Doc helped me into the truck.

"Thanks, man," Doc said.

"No problem." Iggy jogged back into the building and Doc shook his head.

"You need to get a handle on this shit."

"Wherez-bike?" I asked as Doc climbed into the truck beside me.

"Rabbit drove it back to the compound."

"I'm gonna sleep."

"You're not gonna fuckin' sleep, Doom," Doc snapped. "We're gonna get you back to the compound and I'm gonna make sure you don't have a concussion."

"Shul-check-ribs."

"Fuck," Doc ground out. "Yeah, I'll check your ribs."

I chuckled, then coughed, then groaned at the pain.

"Jesus, brother, we gotta have a conversation about this."

"Later."

"Yeah," he said with a sigh. "Always later."

I leaned against the coolness of the window and watched the

street lights whiz by, trying not to pass out again.

* * *

Lyric

Harmony handed me a glass of water and I took a muscle relaxer and a pain pill as she joined me at the kitchen table. "Why are you having Jaxon look into my crash?"

It was well past midnight but I was amped from the night's events and wasn't ready to turn in yet.

Harmony shrugged. "I just have a feeling."

I sighed. "I've always come to fear your 'feelings.' "

She chuckled. "But my feelings are never wrong."

"Which is why I fear them."

"Have you noticed anything weird? Anyone following you? Strange phone calls, stuff like that?"

"No. Nothing." I reached over and squeezed her hand. "He's in jail, Harmony. I know. I check weekly."

"I know. I do, too." She smiled gently. "Jaxon's put everything in the hands of a few of his contacts here and no one's found anything yet, so it's probably nothing. I just wanted every stone unturned, you know?"

"I know, NiNi. Thank you."

She stood and leaned down to kiss my cheek. "Let's get you upstairs."

Before my meds kicked in, Harmony helped me limp up the stairs and then I managed to get myself undressed before falling into bed.

FIVE

Lyric

"WELL, TELL HIM he's an asshole," Melody snapped, and hung up, dropping her phone onto the coffee table.

"Melody!" I admonished. "We weren't raised to speak to people that way."

"Well, he deserves it."

"What's wrong?" Harmony asked, handing Jaxon a beer and sitting beside him on the sofa.

It was the next afternoon and we were enjoying our final day together before Jaxon and Harmony returned to Portland early tomorrow morning.

"Doom was supposed to pick... um... me up for our date tonight," Melody said. "But apparently, he's not coming."

"Oh?" My heart sung, but I stuffed down that emotion and

forced myself to look at my laptop screen. "Did he say why?"

"Oh, he didn't say anything at all," she snapped. "Someone named Doc informed me that he wasn't going to make it."

"That's weird," Jaxon said.

"Why is that weird?" Harmony asked.

Jaxon stood. "Gonna find out. Give me a few."

I glanced at Harmony who shrugged.

Jaxon returned a few minutes later and sat back down. "Yeah, he can't make it."

"Why not?" Harmony asked.

"He just can't."

Harmony turned her body on the sofa to face him. "Again, honey, why not?"

"Let's just say his face wouldn't be very good company."

I frowned, closing my laptop. "What does that mean?"

Jaxon took a swig of his beer.

"Jaxon," Harmony pressed.

"He's got some injuries."

I gasped. "What kind of injuries?"

"The kind that means he can't take Melody out."

"Did he crash his bike?" Harmony asked.

I gasped again. "Oh my god, did he?"

"No," Jaxon said.

"Someone needs to start giving me information, or I swear I'm going to hit something," I warned.

"Not my story to tell," Jaxon said. "Sorry, Lyric."

I picked up my cell phone and swiped the screen, scrolling to Shawn Campbell's number and dialing.

"Hey, Lyric, how are you feeling?"

"I'm doing okay, Shawn, how are you?" I asked.

Shawn Campbell had been my firm's top investigator for over ten years and he was always my first call whenever I needed something fast and accurate.

"Good. What can I do for you?"

"I need information on Lincoln Marxx, two x-es. He's part of the Dogs of Fire motorcycle club and his club name is Doom." I heard Harmony tsk, while Jaxon groaned, but I ignored them both.

"How much information do you need?"

"As much as you can give me," I said.

"Give me a few days."

"Okay, Shawn. Thanks." I hung up and leaned back in my chair with a satisfied smile.

"Major invasion of privacy," Jaxon said, his tone one of caution. "He's not going to like that."

I shrugged and focused back on my screen. "I have an obligation to protect my sister."

"No," Melody rushed to say, which was odd. "You really don't. I don't care. Seriously. It's all good."

"You just called his friend an asshole because Doom couldn't make it," I pointed out.

"Technically, I told him to pass along the message to Doom," Melody countered. "Call Shawn back and cancel your invasion of privacy thing."

"No."

"God! Why do you have to ruin everything?" she snapped, then huffed and stormed out of the room.

"I think you should listen to Melody," Jaxon said. "You dig into information the Dogs haven't offered freely, they won't be happy."

I rolled my eyes. "Are they criminals?"

"Not that anyone has ever been able to prove, no," Jaxon said. "But that doesn't mean they don't have reach, and Doom's not a man to mess with, Lyric."

"No one will ever know what I find out, Jax, especially Doom. You don't have to worry about me."

He raised his hands in surrender. "Okay, babe. Said my piece."

I forced a smile and hoped it appeared genuine. "I appreciate your concern, Jax. I really do. We had to rely on only each other for what felt like forever, so please don't think I take your words lightly."

"As long as you remember I've had your back for a long time and will continue to do so," he said.

"We do, honey," Harmony said, squeezing his knee.

I nodded in agreement.

A little over a week later, life had returned to my new normal. Harmony and Jaxon had returned home, Melody was on the first leg of her sold-out tour, and I was up and moving around a little more, but still on crutches and relying on Uber and coworkers to take me where I needed to go. I hated every second of it. I could not *wait* to get this damn boot off.

I had promised Georgia I'd sit in on one of her other cases at trial this week, the case we had together had been granted a continuance due to my injury, and I was late to the courthouse on account of the fact that I hobbled everywhere right now, so I was not paying attention as I swung my way into the courthouse on Monday morning.

"Shit," a deep voice ground out as I slammed into his hard body.

"Oh, my word, I'm sorry."

"Lyric?"

Doom. I looked up and frowned. "What the hell happened to your face?"

He raised an eyebrow. "You should see the other guy."

"Is this why you canceled your date with my sister?"

"Yeah. Sorry."

He didn't sound sorry in the least bit. "What happened?"

"You late for somethin'?"

"You didn't answer my question," I accused.

"I didn't. You're right, counselor," he said, glancing around. "You should probably get where you need to be, huh?"

"Why are you at court?"

"I had to fight a parking ticket."

I couldn't stop myself from running a finger over one of his bruises. "What did you do?"

He leaned back like my touch burned him. "You need help gettin' where you need to go?"

"No." I cocked my head. "I have a file on you."

Jesus H. Lucifer Christ, why the hell did I just say that out loud?

The darkness I'd grown familiar with covered his face again.

"What?"

"I haven't opened it."

"Fuck me," he growled, and put distance between us.

"I would really like to sit down and have an adult conversation with you and have you tell me your story, rather than reading whatever my investigator found out."

He stepped back to me and leaned close. "Why the fuck do you have a file on me?"

"Because I always do a background check on the men my sisters date."

"I'm not dating your sister."

I raised an eyebrow. "But you will."

"I won't."

"She bid fifty-thousand dollars on you, you don't find that a little bit intriguing?" I challenged.

"No."

"Bullshit."

"Woman, I know everything I need to know about your sister, and no offense, but fucked up, ditzy, and rich enough not to care about anything but herself is not my type." He jabbed a finger toward me. "I will honor my commitment because I don't bail, but no further."

"Contrary to popular belief, my sister isn't actually ditzy."

"Don't give a fuck. Not one single one." He dragged his hands through his hair. "Forget it. Tell your sister I'll refund her fuckin' money, but I'm out. Have a nice life."

He stalked away and I felt like a complete asshole.

I made my way down to the courtroom and took a seat as close to the front as I could, then tried to put my bad behavior aside for the moment.

* * *

"How bad was it?" Georgia asked as we walked out of court.

"What are you talking about?" I countered, sliding my bag over my shoulder. "You did great."

"You must have *some* feedback. I didn't come at Waller hard enough on cross. If it had been you, he would have folded much quicker."

I sighed. "You make me sound like a ball buster."

"Well, you are." She grinned. "In all the best ways."

I rolled my eyes. "Let me think about it and I'll send you an email later today. Honestly, though, I think you have your own style and that works perfectly for you."

She smiled. "Thank you."

"You're welcome."

"Can I drop you somewhere?" she asked.

"No, actually, I need to file a couple of things, so I'll be here for a bit."

She nodded. "Okay, I'll see you on Monday."

My phone rang as Georgia walked away and I saw it was Melody, so I sat on one of the benches and answered it. "Hey, DiDi."

"Hi, how are you?" I could hear noise in the background, so I deduced she was getting ready for a show.

"I'm good, how are you?" I said.

"So good. I met someone."

I rolled my eyes. "Oh?"

"I'll have Brandy send his information so you can do your thing."

I dropped my head back against the wall. "What about Doom?"

"Who?"

"The man you bid fifty-grand on a couple of weeks ago?"

"Oh, him," she said dismissively. "I bid on him for you."

"Excuse me?"

"Yeah. You didn't figure that out?" She chuckled. "He's totally into you, silly. You probably just couldn't see it because of the drugs. I figured I'd just help you jump start some vag action."

"I don't need vag action, sissy," I hiss-pered into the phone, darting my eyes around to make sure no one was listening.

"Yes, you do. It's been, like, forever."

"Okay, my sex life is none of your concern, Melody Dorothy Morgan."

"Okay, *Mom*. Whatever." She laughed outright this time. "I've gotta get back. Just wanted to give you a heads up. Byeeee."

And she was gone. If I hadn't been in public, I think I would have banged my head against something hard. The last thing Melody needed was another man in her life.

And I needed to apologize to the one she'd tried to force into mine.

I wrinkled my nose.

I hated apologizing when I was wrong. I was actually much better at apologizing when I was right.

* * *

Doom

Goddamn fucking bitch! I stalked into the compound and grabbed a bottle of tequila from the bar forgoing a glass.

"Doom!" Rabbit called.

"Fuck off," I snapped, and headed to my room. I didn't get far.

"Doom?"

I slowed my pace at the quiet voice of Alamo's woman, Jasmine, but didn't stop. "Not now, Jazz."

"I'll send Willow," she warned.

I stalled, turning slowly to face her. "What do you want, Jasmine?"

"What happened?"

I could lie and say nothing, but she knew me, so it would be pointless. And if she turned Willow onto me, then all hell would break loose and I'd be fucked. Willow was Dash's woman and she used to be a preacher's daughter. Used to be, only because her father was deceased and she was married to Dash. But she was a quiet force to be reckoned with and had a way of getting information out of me without saying a word. It was uncanny.

"Not really interested in talkin' about it," I said.

"Okay, honey, I get that, but disappearing into your room, alone, with a bottle of tequila isn't really a good idea." She leaned forward. "After you've gone a few rounds with some-one…?"

I'd made a quick stop into Burt's first, but it had been a disappointing detour, so I came back to the club to drink.

"I think it's a phenomenal idea," I countered.

"I'm really concern—"

"Doom!" Alamo bellowed.

I dropped my head back and stared at the ceiling.

"Doom!" Alamo yelled again, this time louder.

"What?" I bellowed back.

"Visitor."

"Jesus Christ," I hissed. "Who is it?"

"Not your secretary, brother."

"Your old man's an asshole," I growled, stalking away from Jasmine.

"No he's not."

"Yes, he is," I argued, hearing her laugh as I walked into the great room and froze. "Oh, hell no. Get her the fuck out of here."

"Wait," Lyric said. "Please. Give me five minutes."

"No."

"Doom, I—"

"Bitch, you better turn your skinny ass around and slink it the fuck out of here—"

"Lincoln, please," she begged.

I squeezed my eyes shut and took a deep breath in an effort not to hit the wall.

"Use my office," Alamo offered.

I scowled at him, but he gave me a chin lift in challenge. I gave him a silent challenge of my own. One that would come in the form of my fist in his face at a time of my choosing. I turned and headed toward Alamo's office, not caring if Lyric followed me or not.

She did, but it took her a minute because she was still on crutches. I should have been a gentleman and helped her, but as I'm sure she'd discovered in her file, I was an asshole and it was important she didn't forget it.

Stepping into the office, I opened the tequila and took a long pull before setting it on Alamo's desk and leaning against the wood. I crossed my arms and waited for Lyric to hobble inside and close the door.

God, she looked gorgeous. She wore a long black and white

striped skirt with a slit that obviously helped her maneuver with her boot. Her tight white T-shirt showcased full tits and she'd left her long, blonde hair to fall like a cascade of spun gold around her shoulders. She had a satchel slung diagonally over her shoulder, and the strap settled between her breasts which drew focus and my dick took notice.

I shook my head. I had to shut this shit down.

"What do you want, Lyric?"

"I...I'm really sorry," she said.

"Yeah?"

"Yes."

"Okay. Great," I said, standing. "Have a nice life."

"I handled today badly," she whispered. "I am so, so sorry." She fumbled with her bag, managing to open it with one hand and pulling out a large manila envelope, thrusting it at me. "Take it. I haven't even looked at it. I have no idea what's in it. You could be a serial killer for all I know. Or a gigolo." She wrinkled her nose. "But, honestly, I don't know which one would be worse to have on your record."

I couldn't deal with her beautiful mouth forming words anymore, especially when her eyes grew a little misty and the sincerity of her apology went straight to my dick. I closed the distance between us and covered her mouth with mine, my hand sliding to her neck and stroking her pulse as I deepened the kiss.

Jesus, she tasted like a fuckin' mint julep. Southern belle to the core.

I heard the clatter of her crutches hitting the floor and she gripped my cut as she held on for dear life, mewing quietly before breaking the kiss. "Oh my god."

Fuck.

"Does that mean I'm forgiven?" she rasped.

"No."

She met my eyes. "Do you really think I have a skinny ass?"

"No."

She sighed. "Good. I spend a shit ton of time at the gym getting that butt...well, I did before the accident. I was nervous it was disappearing."

"It's not."

"Glad you noticed."

"Are you fucking seriously saying that right now?"

She shrugged. "Well, now that I'm forgiven, I figured we could have a more lighthearted conversation."

"You're not forgiven."

She smiled. "Yes, I am."

"How do you figure?"

"You kissed me."

"I'm a gigolo. I kiss a lot of women."

She raised an eyebrow. "Oh, ho, so now we're finally sharing personal information."

"That's not really personal information."

"Okay, well, I'd like to use your services, but I'm not going to actually pay you any money. I mean, *technically*, my sister has already procured you."

"Excuse me?"

"Oh, right, you don't know. Melody bid on you so I'd get some 'vag action.' And I realized today, she might be right, so I'd like to fuck you."

"Jesus Christ, Lyric, no way in hell." If she'd been able to stand on her own two feet, I would have put as much distance between us as possible, but I couldn't in good conscience walk away and chance her falling.

"Why not?"

I guided her to a chair and helped her sit down and then walked to the other side of the office. "Because I'm not the committing kind."

"I'm not looking for a commitment."

"Baby, a woman like you is *always* looking like a commitment."

She frowned. "What the hell is that supposed to mean?"

"High class is always looking for commitment and you're that in spades, Angel. You deserve nothing less. Someone to grow old with, kids, the whole nine."

She smiled. "I appreciate that, Lincoln, but I'm not looking for commitment. It brings strings I don't really want. I can't have kids, so they have never been on the radar for me—"

"Why can't you have kids?"

"Old injury."

"What kind of injury would make you unable to have a kid?"

"I was stabbed."

"What the fuck?" I snapped.

She waved her hand dismissively. "It was a long time ago, Lincoln. It's done. I'm looking for stress relief and a little levity when I have a hard case. Or several orgasms when I want to bury a client. I work in a very small town and gossip runs rampant, so it would be nice to get that distraction outside of my current sphere of influence. So. Will you be my stress reliever?"

"No."

"Are you already dating someone?" she asked, then frowned. "Although, why would you kiss me if you're with someone else?"

"No."

"Okay, so if you're free, be free with me."

"That's not what I meant," I countered. "Who got you the file on me?"

"My investigator."

"And what's he gonna do with the information?"

"Nothing."

"How do you know?"

"Well, for one, he doesn't store anything he gets for me. Unlike my counterparts, I don't like digital footprints, so he prints everything out, pretty much without looking at it…much, anyway. He throws it into a file and hands it over." She shrugged. "I mean, I suppose it isn't outside the realm of possibility that he might save searches and such, but, unless you're someone he needs to get something from, I can't imagine why he would. This was a personal, off the books request."

I scowled. "Don't like people knowing my business, Lyric."

"No one does. I mean, at least, that you don't want to."

"Sounds like your man does."

"If he knows anything, he won't say a word. I would stake my life on it."

She was so sincere, I almost believed her. Almost. But the problem with believing people who were sincere is that it got your world fucked up.

"Well, let's hope you're right."

"I am," she said. "So, now that that's out of the way…"

I shook my head. "We're not going to do this."

She shrugged. "Why not?"

"Because it's not a good idea, Lyric."

"I disagree. I think it's a great idea, Lincoln." She rose to her feet and hopped toward me. I sighed and closed the distance between us, reaching for her so she didn't fall. "It's just sex, Doom. A little fun. Two gorgeous people in the prime of their life gettin' a little. We can end it anytime. No harm, no foul."

"Don't want to hurt you, Lyric."

She slid her hand under my T-shirt. "No harm, no foul, Lincoln."

Lyric

 IS MOUTH COVERED mine again, and I slid my hands under his T-shirt and up his muscular back. Oh my god, I wanted to breathe every bit of his essence into my body.

Breaking the kiss, I gripped his vest. "I really, really want to give you a blow job, but I need your help to do it."

He raised an eyebrow, his eyes growing dark. "I don't have any condoms with me."

"Well, where are they?"

"In my room."

I bit my lip. "Take me to your room."

He squeezed his eyes shut. "Fuck."

"Please."

He cupped my face. "You really wanna do this?"

"Yes."

He stroked my cheek. "Can you maneuver stairs?"

"Slowly, but, yes." I nodded toward the desk. "Bring the tequila."

"Is that a good idea?"

"I've only had Tylenol today, so it's a very good idea."

He grinned, handing me my crutches, then grabbing the bottle of tequila and my bag. "We'll go slow."

"Okay, but only if you promise we'll go fast later."

He studied me for a second. "You're gonna be a problem, aren't you?"

"If you're lucky, yes."

He smiled and I almost lost my breath. It was the first time I'd ever seen him smile and it was absolutely magnificent. Wrapping an arm around my waist, he helped me up the stairs and down a long hallway to a large wooden door. He unlocked it and pushed it open, flipping on a light and helping me inside, then kicking the door shut before kissing me again.

"Are you clean?" I asked.

"Yes. Are you?"

"Yes. I have the proof in my bag."

"Seriously?"

I nodded. "I brought it…in case."

"Well, if we're gettin' all that shit out on the table, I've got mine as well."

We exchanged information, while taking a few sips from the tequila bottle, then I said boldly, "Um, if you're okay with it, I'd like no condoms."

He closed his eyes and took a deep breath. "Fuck me."

"Yes, exactly."

He met my eyes. "If that's the case, we're exclusive."

"That sounds like a commitment, Lincoln."

"I don't share, Lyric."

"Again, that sounds like commitment," I pointed out.

"Well, then, what do you suggest?"

"How about we agree that you glove up if you decide you want to sleep with anyone else and I'll do the same."

His eyes danced with humor. "You'll glove up?"

I smiled. "Yep. I'll use a big ol' female condom."

"I can get behind that."

"Good. Now, I'd like to wrap my mouth around what I'm sure will be an incredibly beautiful dick, so how about you strip and I'll sit myself down in that chair over there."

"How about I make you feel good first?"

"You will, provided you get your clothes off, pronto."

"You always this bossy?" he asked, running a finger over my jawline.

"I was the youngest partner in my law firm, so, yes."

"Yeah? Were you also the bad girl of your class? You like to role play, Angel? How about I be opposing counsel and show you my briefs?"

"I'd rather you be the judge, so take out your gavel and get to banging." I waved a finger toward his dick. "Now, free the peen."

He chuckled, removing his vest and throwing it on the bed before pulling off his T-shirt.

"Wait," I demanded, and crooked my finger. "Come closer for a second."

"Lyr—"

"Hush." I laid my fingers over his lips and his beard tickled my palm. "I just want to look at you."

His right arm was covered with tattoos, but his left was bare, which I found sexy as hell. He had a Dogs of Fire logo across his rib cage and I ran a finger over it, his abs contracting as I did. His muscles had muscles and my tongue fully planned to follow the sinewy map as far as it went.

"You are a beautiful man, Lincoln."

"Thanks, Angel."

"I want to see the rest."

"Quid pro quo, Lyric."

"Huh-uh. My money, my time," I argued.

"I told you I'm payin' that back."

"No, you're not. The check has already cleared and Melody doesn't want the money," I said, tugging at the waistband of his jeans, unbuttoning them and lowering the zipper. "She would have donated it outright, anyway."

Doom slid his arm around my waist and walked me backwards to the chair, helping me sit down, then removing the rest of his clothes.

"Lordy," I breathed out at the sight of his cock. "*That* is perfect." I licked my lips and wrapped my hand around its girth. He stepped closer and I ran my tongue up the length then wrapped my mouth around the tip, taking him deeper and deeper until his dick touched the back of my throat. I could *not* get enough.

"Jesus Christ," he hissed. "You need to slow down, Angel, or I'm gonna come."

I pulled back, releasing him with a smack. "How long does it take you to recover?"

"Not long."

"Then, come when you want to come." I took his cock back in my mouth and took him deep again, sucking and moving my hands in time with my mouth. God, he tasted incredible.

His fingers slid into my hair and his hands gripped my scalp as he began to fuck my face, then his body locked and I knew he was close.

"Now, Angel," he rasped, and I gripped his legs as he exploded in my mouth.

I took every drop and swallowed as he cupped my face, leaning down to kiss me. "Amazing."

"Agreed." I ran my tongue over my lips. "I could spend my day feasting on you."

"Good to know." He chuckled. "Your turn."

I smiled. "Okay."

He helped me up, sliding my T-shirt over my head, then removing my bra. I had to hold onto his waist to keep my balance.

"You good?" he asked.

"Yep."

"You need to get off that leg?"

"Not yet. I'll tell you."

"Okay, Angel." He bent down and drew a nipple into his mouth biting gently, then blowing. I slid my fingers into his hair and gripped his scalp.

He kissed his way down my belly, kneeling in front of me

and sliding my skirt down my legs, leaving me in just my panties and boot.

"Don't get too turned on by the boot, Doom. I was warned it can make a man come in five-point-two."

"I'll do my best." He chuckled, burying his face between my legs, his mouth covering my mound over my panties.

Hooking his fingers under the waistband, he slid them down my thighs, maneuvered them over my boot and threw them in the corner, then his mouth was back to its task and his beard was adding to the sensation. I dropped my head back. God, this was amazing. I'd never even kissed anyone with a beard, so this was magical. He ran a tongue over my clit, then between my already wet folds and I gripped his scalp again in an effort to stay upright.

"I don't think I'll be able to stay upright with you doing that," I admitted.

He smiled, standing, then lifted me onto the bed gently. Grabbing a couple of pillows, he settled my booted leg over it, leaving my other leg free and I couldn't help covering my face with my hands.

"What are you doing?" he asked.

"I feel like I'm getting ready for a pap smear."

"Jesus, Angel, don't say that. I'm known around the world for my prowess, don't limit me to a minor gynecologist."

I leaned up on my arms. "Prowess?"

"So much prowess." He pushed gently on my chest. "Relax."

I laid back down and he covered my core with his mouth again. I slid my fingers into his hair as he sucked my clit, then dipped his tongue inside of me, and I couldn't really think because I was floating on air.

He sucked, licked, and fingered me to one of the most amazing orgasms I'd ever had, but before I came down, he hovered over me, smiling before kissing me and sliding into me slowly.

"Good?"

"Oh, God, yes," I breathed out, sliding my hands up his back.

His hand slid to my neck and he kissed me again. "If you need to stop, tell me."

"Okay," I whispered, wrapping my good leg around his waist as he moved.

And, lord, he *moved*, slowly at first, letting me get used to his size and adjust to the strange angle I was in with my gimpy leg. I savored the feel of him inside of me, one hand at my neck, the other rolling a nipple into a tight bead.

"You're beautiful, Lyric," Doom whispered, kissing me again.

"You certainly make me feel that way. Boot and all."

"Oh, the boot adds to the sex appeal."

I grinned.

"You ready?" he asked.

"So ready."

He buried himself again, then slammed into me over and over, careful to baby my leg while still managing to hit my g-spot. A second orgasm built and a climax washed over me just as his cock pulsed inside of me.

I arched against him, weaving my fingers into his hair as my body shuddered with release.

"Wow," he rasped, running his nose against mine.

"Wow, indeed," I agreed.

He slid out of me, climbing off the bed and stepping into the bathroom attached to his bedroom. He returned with a warm washcloth and cleaned me up before throwing the terrycloth into the corner and stretching out beside me. "How's your leg?"

"It's actually good."

"You up for another round?"

"I don't have time, actually. Sorry. I have some work I need to get done."

"I'll take you home."

"No, it's fine. I'll get an Uber. I kind of derailed your night."

"It's all good, Lyric. I can take you home."

"I can't get on a bike with this boot, Doom."

"I can borrow Alamo's truck," he countered, grabbing his discarded clothing from the floor.

"Don't go to the trouble," I said, and started to get dressed.

"Seriously. I'll grab an Uber. It's all good. You looked like you were about to have some fun, so do that."

I smiled and gathered my things, sliding my foot into my single flip flop.

* * *

Doom

"Text me when you get home," I said.

"I will," she promised. "Thanks for the stress relief. I needed it."

"Me too, Angel." I helped Lyric into the Uber, kissed her one more time, then headed back into the compound.

"What the fuck is this?" Alamo growled, holding the manila envelope Lyric brought with her in the air. I forgot I left it in his office. Not surprising. I was a little distracted.

"Don't know," I admitted. "I haven't looked at it."

"Well, let me enlighten you. It's your life. The whole fuckin' shebang," he said. "Shit I'm pretty sure only Doc and I know."

I dragged my hands down my face. Shit.

"What I want to know is why is it in a sealed envelope in my office?" Alamo continued.

"Lyric did a background check."

His mouth dropped open. "And she's still alive?" he asked somewhat sarcastically.

"She didn't look at it."

"She had you investigated, but didn't look at the infor-mation?"

I nodded, crossing my arms. "That's what she said."

Alamo sighed. "Brother, are you sure this is a good idea?"

"No clue."

He shook his head and handed me the envelope. "Just go easy, okay? I swear to Christ, if I have to turn Willow on to you, it's not gonna be pretty."

"Jesus, why do y'all threaten to sic her on me?"

"Because she's the only one who can get through to you when you go dark."

I flipped him off and headed to the kitchen for coffee, my mind turning to Lyric. Fuck, she was incredible. I had to force myself not to rage at the sight of the scars across her abdomen.

Nine of them. They were faint and by no means took away from the beauty of her body, but they were there and they were the evidence of the trauma that took away her ability to have children.

Jesus Christ, what kind of monster could do that?

This was exactly what I intended to find out.

* * *

Lyric

I arrived home and flopped onto my sofa, my body still thrumming from the best sex of my life. God, I had no idea sex could be like that. I mean, I'd had good sex, I'd had bad sex, but I'd never had mind-numbing sex.

My phone buzzed in my purse and I dug it out to see Wes calling. I hadn't heard from him in a while, so I hoped nothing was wrong. "Hi, Wes."

"Hey, Lyric. Did I catch you at a bad time?"

Loaded question, buddy.

"No, not at all. Is everything okay with Sutter Street?"

"I'm not calling about business."

"Oh, okay."

"Are you seeing anyone?"

That depends. Am I seeing him naked? Yes. Am I dating him? No.

"No one exclusively," I said. "Why?"

"I'd like to take you out."

"On a date?"

"Yes. Roller skating."

"Wes—"

"Kidding," he said, and chuckled. "The case is done and my invoice has been paid, which means we're no longer professionally linked, so I'd like to take you on a real date and get to know you."

"Um…"

"Dinner, somewhere with no stairs. I'll pick you up and we'll go at your pace. Saturday night?"

"You know, Saturday night's prime date night time," I pointed out.

"I'm aware, which is why I asked you if you were seeing anyone."

"It's kind of short notice."

Wes chuckled. "Lyric, I know you well enough to know that if you had a date, you'd come right out and say it. So, unless you find me grotesque, which I know you don't, I'll pick you up at seven—"

"I like to eat like a geriatric."

"Okay, I'll pick you up at four."

"Maybe more like a senior citizen."

"Five-thirty. We'll head to the Chart House."

I let out a quiet gasp. "I love the Chart House."

"I'm aware."

It was my favorite restaurant. I'd taken his team there when we'd won the case and probably mentioned it a thousand times.

I smiled. He remembered.

"I'll be ready," I said.

"Great. See you then."

He hung up and I dropped my head back. Well, now my life was suddenly getting very, very interesting.

SEVEN

Lyric

A T THREE A.M. Saturday morning, I awoke in pain. More pain than should be normal. I sat up and forced my legs over the side of my bed, panting from the strain. I knew I'd probably just slept weird and needed to get up so I could get the blood flowing right again, but I just couldn't.

This was the downside of being the cat lady who lived alone. No one would find me for days if I died. Oh, and my cat would eat my corpse.

I took a deep breath and forced myself to put pressure on my foot, crying out when the pain registered all the way to my hip. Booger meowed and meandered over to me, rubbing his head on my arm, obviously wondering why the hell I was awake at such an ungodly hour.

Or he was tenderizing me in prep for his meal later.

"Meow."

"Not today, Satan. Not today."

I took another deep breath and put more pressure on it and even worse pain shot through my body. I didn't know what to do. Melody was in Phoenix, Harmony was in Portland, and I had no other family. It's not like I could call Wes. We were about to go on our first date tonight, and I just, I don't know, didn't really know him, so I grabbed my phone and chose to make a bad decision. I called Doom. He answered immediately.

"Lyric, you okay?"

"No," I rasped. "Something's wrong with my leg." I took a deep breath. "It really hurts."

"Okay, baby, don't move. I'll be right there."

He hung up and I sat at the edge of the bed and tried to breathe through the pain, feeling like someone was shoving spikes into my shin. I wanted to adjust my boot, but knew if I tried, I'd probably just fuck things up even more, so I stayed as still as I could and waited. I wish I'd kept a bottle of pain pills next to the bed.

Twenty minutes later, Doom arrived and I used my app to open the garage for him so he could get into the house. It didn't dawn on me to question how he knew where I lived, probably because I couldn't really think about anything but the pain. Doom walked in with a man I'd never seen before which kind of freaked me out and I let out a quiet squeak.

"Who the hell are you?" I snapped, trying to pull my covers over my half-dressed body.

"Lyric, this is Doc. He's our club president, and he's also a doctor. I asked him to come and check you out."

"You're really a doctor?"

"Yes," he said, turning on the lamp next to my bed, then kneeling beside me. "Get the ceiling light, Doom," he directed.

"Switch is on the wall," I said.

Doom turned on the light and Doc gently slid the boot off my foot. "Pretty painful, huh?"

I nodded, biting back tears.

"This is good, Lyric. Your leg's doing what it's supposed to be doing, but that means you're gonna feel all of those nerves as they come back to life."

"So it's not going to kill me?"

"No. The boot twisted a bit, so your leg moved inside of it and got pinched. Nothing damaging." He adjusted the boot and I felt some relief, letting out a breath I didn't realize I'd been holding. "Better?"

"Yes, actually. Thank you."

He gave me a gentle smile. "You should take something a little stronger than Tylenol. Do you need me to write you a script?"

I shook my head. "I still have pain meds."

"Okay, babe. Take a dose and you should be good."

I sniffed and bit my lip. "Thank you. I thought I'd done something really bad to it."

"I'm sure it hurt like a mother fucker, but you're all good. I'm gonna leave you, but if you need anything, let Doom know, okay?"

I nodded. "Thanks. I really appreciate it."

"No problem."

He grabbed his bag, nodded to Doom, and walked out the door.

I burst into tears and Doom walked over to me and wrapped me in a hug.

"Oh my god, I can't believe you came all the way over here when I called," I said.

"Baby, we might not be exclusive, but we're becomin' friends, so that makes you club business."

"And that's a good thing?" I asked.

"Well, it is if it means you're in pain and need help at three o'clock in the mornin'."

"Thank you," I whispered.

"You're welcome." He lifted my chin. "Where are your meds?"

"In the kitchen, above the dishwasher."

"Okay, I'll go find them. You want me to stay or head back to the club?"

"Will you stay?"

"Sure."

He kissed me gently, then went and got my meds.

* * *

I rolled over and my face connected with a very muscular chest and I forgot for half a second that Doom was in my bed. Then I smiled. Doom was in my bed.

"Mornin', Angel."

"Are you naked?"

He chuckled. "Not quite."

I met his eyes. "Shame."

Before he could comment, Booger jumped onto the bed and promptly settled himself on top of Doom's head. Doom grinned, reaching up to pet my cat, taking all of it in stride. "I take it this is where he normally sleeps?"

"Yes. Unless he's sleeping on *my* head." I met his eyes. "How did you know where I lived?"

"I have my own guy," he said evasively. "How's your leg?"

"So much better." I kissed his chest. "Thank you again for coming to my rescue. I didn't know who else to call."

His mood shifted suddenly, I could feel it because his body stiffened. Minutely, maybe, but enough for me to notice. Before I could ask why, however, he gave my bottom a gentle smack and climbed out of bed. "Got shit to do today, how about I make you breakfast before I head out?"

"Ah…sure."

He headed to my bathroom and I sat up and slid my legs over the side of the mattress. When he walked back into my room, I met his eyes. "Do me a favor."

"What do you need?"

"If I do or say something that pisses you off, promise me you'll tell me," I said. "Don't ghost me. I like you. I like the friendship we're building. I love the sex. I don't want anything else, but if we decide to stop doing this, I want it to be mutual and friendly. Not because of some invisible slight."

He crossed his arms. "I can do that."

I nodded. "Good. Now, I want bacon and French toast with really strong coffee. So, I'm going to shower while you make that."

"You need help?"

I shook my head. "I've pretty much got this down to a science now, but thanks."

After my shower, I hobbled downstairs and into my kitchen to find a note on my fridge.

Breakfast is in the oven, coffee's in the pot. Had shit to do. D.

I grabbed an oven mitt and pulled it out, made a cup of coffee, then grabbed my phone and called my sister while I ate.

"Hey, LiLi. To what do I owe this early morning call?"

"Shit, NiNi, I'm sorry!" I groaned. "I totally didn't think."

"I'm just giving you a hard time. I was already up. Are you okay?"

"I have a date."

"That's awesome. With Doom?"

"No."

"Oh, wait, what?" she said, then slightly off the speaker, "No, honey, you're not wearing that. I don't care if aunty Melody wears it onstage, you are not thirty and desperate for male attention."

"Mom!" Skyler whined. "I'm the only one who doesn't get to dress the way she wants to."

"That's complete bull and you know it."

"But—"

"Go put on proper clothes or I'll have your dad pick out an outfit for you."

"You're so unfair!" Skyler snapped.

"And it's why you won't be murdered and stuffed into a barrel on my watch." This was said very quietly so only I could hear.

"Oh my god," I said, trying not to laugh. "When the hell did she turn into DiDi?"

"Two years ago. She's a monster, LiLi," Harmony whispered. "And I was the good sister, for Pete's sake. If Mel has kids, she's probably going to get some quiet, sweet child who doesn't say boo."

"You might have been quiet and sweet, but you said boo. You are also changing the world and Skyler will too."

"God, you always know what to say." She sighed. "You would have made the best mom."

I bit back sadness. "I'll just relish being the best aunty on the planet."

"Right. So, who's getting your hoo-ha tonight?"

"Um, no one. But Wes is taking me to the Chart House."

"Whoa, the guy's serious if he's taking you to the Chart House."

"He's certainly bringing his A-game," I said.

"Wes was the guy we met at the dinner, right?" she asked.

"Yes."

"Oh, he was nice."

I smiled. "Yeah, he's a good guy."

"And really good looking."

I chuckled. "Yes, he's that as well."

"What happened with Doom?"

"What do you mean?"

"Well, Melody paid for a date with him, so are you going to go out with him?"

"Maybe," I said evasively. "But I should probably focus on Wes first, huh?"

"Probably," she conceded. "What are you going to wear?"

"That's kind of why I called…"

* * *

Wes arrived promptly at five-thirty and I pulled the door open to find him holding a beautiful bouquet of wild flowers. "Hi. Come in."

"You look beautiful," he said, leaning down to kiss my cheek and handing me the flowers.

I wore a sleeveless, denim blue maxi dress, gathered at the waist with a split up the side that gave me ample room to accommodate my boot. I had one blingy flat sandal on that matched my clutch and I'd pulled my hair into a high ponytail so my large hoop earrings could be seen.

"Thank you. You look great as well."

Wes wore dark jeans and a black button up, open at the throat with a fitted dinner jacket. He wore a pair of snakeskin shoes that were cool as all get out…and kind of his 'thing.'

"I'll get these in water and we can go."

"How about I carry those," he suggested and I smiled.

"Good plan."

I led him into the kitchen, propped my crutches against the counter, and grabbed a vase, filling it with water while he unwrapped the flowers and set them inside.

"Thanks," I said. "Ready?"

"Ready."

Grabbing my crutches, purse, and keys, I followed him outside and locked the door, then he helped me down my front steps and into his Mercedes, before climbing into the driver's side and pulling out of my driveway. I did have a kneeling scooter-thingy, but it just felt way too old-lady for a date night, so I opted to use my crutches instead.

Because of my boot, I had been granted a temporary disabled placard, so we were able to park in a handicapped spot. Wes helped me out of the car and led me into the restaurant, making sure doors were opened and seats were cleared while we waited, briefly, for our table.

The hostess led us to a romantic table by the window with an unobstructed view of the water. The sun was just beginning to set and it was perfect. Wes held my chair while I settled myself, then he took his seat and the hostess handed us our menus.

I promptly set mine aside and Wes chuckled. "You know what you want, huh?"

"Always."

"Filet mignon, medium rare?"

I raised an eyebrow. "How could you possibly remember my order?"

"I pay attention when I'm interested in someone or something."

"Charmer."

He chuckled. Dinner progressed with easy conversation and light flirting, but I found my mind often turning to Doom, which I found disconcerting. It was probably just the lingering effects of the orgasm he gave me. I more than likely just needed another one to get him out of my system.

EIGHT

Lyric

FIVE MONDAYS LATER, I walked into my house and discovered not one, but two of my kitchen light-bulbs were out. Shit like this always happened at the worst time. You know, like when you break your leg and can't climb a ladder.

I limped into the parlor and unplugged a couple of my lamps, transferring one to my dinette and the other to my kitchen island. It wasn't a permanent fix, but it helped. I'd just opened my fridge to figure out what to make for dinner when my phone rang. It was Doom.

"Well, hi there," I said, my heart racing in a really good way. We'd been on a good sex schedule so far. Monday, Friday, and sometimes Sunday or Tuesday depending on the week. I don't know why I didn't make a deal like this ages ago.

"Hey, babe, you up for some relief?" Doom asked.

I bit my lip. "Well, that depends."

"On?"

"How do you feel about heights?"

"Used to be a firefighter, Angel, heights aren't a problem."

"Right. Well, I've got a couple of bulbs out in my kitchen ceiling and I can't climb a ladder right now…"

He chuckled. "No problem. I'll screw them, then you. See you in a few."

"Okay," I breathed out.

He arrived twenty minutes later and came in through my garage. He greeted me with a sexy as fuck kiss, making me want to throw him on my kitchen floor and fuck him right there and then.

Damn boot.

"Hey, beautiful."

"Hi," I said with a sigh. "You smell good."

"Yeah?"

"Like the woods."

"Irish Spring."

I chuckled. "You showered with the fancy soap?"

"I showered with the fancy soap on a *rope*."

"Wow, I feel special."

"You should." He kissed me again. "Now, where are the replacement lightbulbs and shit?"

"Everything's in the garage. Want me to order a pizza?"

"Pizza'd be good. Pepperoni, olive, and mushroom."

"Okay."

While Doom took care of my lights, I took care of our food. Everything took less than half an hour, which meant we were at my kitchen island with pizza and beer eating under bright lights and laughing at the look of horror on the pizza guy's face when Doom had threatened to introduce his face to the pavement.

"I really shouldn't laugh," I said. "He was young and he was trying to flirt."

"He was a classic predator, preyin' on what I'm sure he hoped was a single woman alone."

"Wow, you sound like Harmony."

"Yeah, well, she would know." He took a swig of beer, then met my eyes. "You need to be careful, Angel."

"I am, Doom. Promise." I leaned my chin in my palm. "Why do you call me Angel?"

His mouth twitched. "Got my reasons."

"Okay." I rolled my eyes. "So, you used to be a firefighter and now you own a body shop, right?"

"You really didn't read that file, did you?"

"I told you I didn't."

"A lot of people tell me lots of things, Lyric. Don't mean they're not lyin'."

"I will never lie to you, Lincoln. I might not always be able to tell you things, for obvious reasons, but I'll never lie."

He cocked his head. "Crazy as this sounds, but I believe you."

"So," I prodded. "Firefighter…"

"Ah, yeah, was a firefighter. Decided I didn't want to do it anymore. Opened a body shop next to Alamo's. He's a mechanic."

"Don't you need training?"

He stared at me for a few seconds and I stared back.

"I'm not asking for your heart's secrets, Lincoln. I'm trying to get to know the man who's shoving his incredibly large dick inside my vagina."

He dropped his head back and laughed and I swear, said vagina tingled with need.

"Okay, let me see." He wiped his mouth and tapped his fingers on the kitchen island. "I've always tinkered with cars. My uncle was a mechanic and he taught me to fix pretty much everything, but I was that artsy kid who painted and shit, so he helped me focus on the body side of it. My dad does construction and I worked construction with him most summers. It was a chance to get out of the house and spend time with him. On weekends, I'd work with my uncle. Then, senior year, a friend's house burned down, everyone was okay, but he and I were jacked up on adrenaline and the need to be heroes, so we decided to go into the fire academy together. I worked with my dad on

66

my days off helping my friend's family rebuild the house, then I worked for the fire department until… well, until I was done and now I do this."

"Are you and your dad still close?"

"Story time's over," he said, sliding off his stool. "Now it's time for me to shove my incredibly large dick into your already wet pussy."

"You don't know it's already wet."

"Oh, it's already wet."

He helped me up the stairs and kissed me as he removed my clothes, lifting me gently onto the bed. "Can't wait for you to get that boot off, Angel."

"You and me both, bud."

He helped position my leg over the pillows and made sure I was comfortable. "Yeah, but I bet not for the same reasons."

I raised an eyebrow as he removed his clothes. "Do tell."

"I'm ready to fuck you in all manner of different positions."

I shivered. "Doom! Why do you say things like that when there's nothing you can do about them? It's mean. Nay, it's bordering on cruel and unusual punishment."

"Oooh, are you going to slap me with a tort?"

I laughed. "Ah, that's not really how that works."

"Slapping me with any kind of pie works, baby. But right now, I'm interested in some honey," he said, burying his face in my pussy.

I gripped his head and dug my heel into the mattress to keep my body from floating off the bed, arching into his mouth. God, I wish I could use my other leg.

"Doom, now. Don't make me wait."

He smiled up at me. "Eager, Angel?"

I let out a frustrated growl in answer and he laughed, crawling up my body and sliding into me. Slowly. Jerk.

"Lincoln," I warned.

He kissed me, putting me out of my misery and buried himself deeper inside of me, then he moved, slamming into me harder and harder until I came so hard, I screamed his name.

"Now that I'm deaf…," he rasped, running his nose against mine.

"Whatever. You loved every second."

He chuckled and kissed me gently, then slid out of me, pulling me against his chest. "Do you have a date to get the boot off yet?"

"About three more weeks."

"You let me know and I'll go with you."

"Okay."

Doom ran a finger over one of my scars and asked, "You feel like sharin'?"

"You didn't find everything out you wanted to know when you did your background check?"

"I saw the police report, yes. But I didn't go medical records deep."

"I was right out of law school, working for the DA's office and Garrett Smalls was being prosecuted for rape, kidnapping, and murder. We had him dead to rights on everything, but I still wanted to make sure no rock was left unturned. Which meant, I was on his radar. Long story short, he made bail. His grandmother's loaded and she got him out. I was supposed to have a detail on me twenty-four-seven, but he got to me during the shift change."

Doom pulled me a little closer and I closed my eyes, the memories flooding back.

"He stabbed me in my abdomen nine times before he was pulled off of me. Irreparable damage to my uterus, but otherwise, no major organs hit. Lucky to be alive, yada yada."

"I'm sorry, Angel."

I forced a smile and glanced up at him. "It sucked. Big time. But I couldn't dwell in what could have been and wasn't, or I'd have curled up and died. I have a great life and an incredible career, and now I have my sexual needs tended to, so what's not to be thankful for?"

Doom chuckled, rolling me onto my back and kissing me. "Your sexual needs are tended to, huh?"

"Quite nicely, yes."

"I'd appreciate it if you'd leave me a good review on Yelp."

"Yelp does reviews for gigolos?"

"Yelp does reviews for *everything*," he retorted, kissing me.

I chuckled, stroking his beard. "I have a loaded question for you."

He sighed, closing his eyes. "What?"

"Quinlan's invited me out for girls' night Friday night."

"Quinlan McKellar?" he said in surprise.

"Um, sure? I knew her when she was with Michael. But we reconnected at the benefit dinner and she said she'd invite me out next girls' night. I know Alamo's wife will be there, along with a few of the others from your club and I don't think they know we're... you know."

He rolled off me and onto his back. "No, they don't."

"So, before I say yes, I want to make sure it's not a conflict for you."

"You do whatever you want to do, Lyric," he said, sliding off the bed. "I don't really give a fuck."

"Whoa," I snapped, sitting up. "Where did that come from?"

"I don't like people knowin' my business."

I nodded. "Yes. I'm aware."

"Especially not my brothers' women."

"Lincoln, I wasn't planning on telling them about our arrangement. I just wanted to make sure it wasn't going to make you uncomfortable." I slid off the mattress. "Somewhere along the way, you've gotten the impression that it's okay to speak to me that way. It's not. If you're not willing to have an adult conversation with me, I'd like you to leave."

He snagged his clothes off the floor. "Fine."

He dressed quickly and headed for the door.

"Thanks for changing my lightbulbs," I said quietly.

He paused, lowered his head, then moved right on out my bedroom door and didn't look back. Jebus, I thought women were moody.

* * *

Friday night arrived and I got dressed with both nervous excitement and trepidation. I hadn't had one text from Doom all week, and there was no way in hell I was going to text him. He was obviously pissed about something, but I had no idea what. So much for not ghosting me.

Wes had called on Tuesday to schedule another date for Saturday, so I had to make sure I didn't push my limit tonight with alcohol. The last thing I needed was a hangover while I was out with Wes.

I decided to wear the same dress I'd worn on my date with Wes last time to girls' night. It was super comfortable and it hid my boot, plus, I felt cute in it.

Quin offered to pick me up, so I was excited to have the freedom to drink a little more than I might normally on a night out.

Quin arrived right as I secured my watch and I opened the door and grinned. "Hi."

"Hi," she said, hugging me. "You look gorgeous."

"So do you." She wore dark skinny jeans and black booties with an off the shoulder blouse that fit snugly around her trim waist. Her long, dark hair was pulled up at the sides and she'd kept her makeup light. "Come in for a second. I'm just throwing a few things in my purse."

"I remember when this place was on the market," she said, closing the door behind her. "You've done wonders with it."

My home was less than a block from Forsyth Park, in the historic district, and I loved it. It had been built in 1860 and had been a wreck, but I'd spent two years restoring it to its current beauty and it was now worth four times what I paid for it fifteen years ago. It didn't really matter, I can't imagine ever selling it.

"Thank you. It's absolutely my dream house."

"I can see why."

"Okay, I'm ready," I said, grabbing my bag.

"Let's go." She grinned. "The girls are dying to meet you."

"Let me guess. Because I'm Melody Morgan's sister?"

"What? No!" She frowned. "Oh, my god. I didn't even think about that. People must do that all the time, huh?"

"More than you know." I led her out the front door and locked it.

"Ugh. People suck." She helped me maneuver into her car, then climbed in herself.

"Yes, people do suck."

She wrinkled her nose and started the car. "Well, I'm sorry

people use you to get to your sister. The women you'll meet tonight don't give a rat's ass about your sister, no offense. They'll get to know you based on you and like you or not like you because of who you are. There's no bullshit."

"Well, that sounds refreshing."

She grinned. "It really is. Being with Michael all those years was a nightmare, and I wasted so much time, but now that I'm finally with Knox, life is finally right and I'm part of a world where I fit."

I smiled. "That's all you could ever ask for, right?"

"Exactly."

The restaurant-slash-bar where we were meeting everyone wasn't far from my house and since I had my handicap placard, we were able to park right in front.

"Ooh, I might need to take you shopping while you have that thing on," Quin said.

I chuckled. "Name the day and time and I'm yours."

Quin grabbed my crutches from the backseat while I slid out of the car, then I got myself situated and followed her inside.

"Girl, get your ass over here," Jasmine Slater called. "You're late!"

Quin laughed. "By four minutes."

"Liv's already three Lemon Drops in—"

"Four," the brunette woman to her left corrected.

"Really, honey?" Jasmine asked gently. "Do you think you might want to slow down?"

"Barkeep, I'd like another!" Liv called.

Jasmine gave Quin some kind of look and Quin nodded. "Lyric, have a seat. I'll be right back."

I nodded and took a seat while Quin made her way to the bar, returning with what looked like a lemon drop and handing it to Liv. "Here you go, honey."

"I love you, thank you."

She smiled, and leaned over to me. "Majorly watered down."

"Ah."

"Lyric, that's Willow, she's Dash's wife, you met Jasmine at the benefit, and drinking the lemon drop is Olivia. She's... well, she's Doc's... um..."

"Friend," Olivia provided.

"Sure, we'll go with that," Quin said.

"And I'm Parker. I'm Jasmine's secret lover."

"She wishes," Jasmine retorted.

I laughed. "Well, hi, Parker, it's nice to meet you."

A cocktail waitress arrived and took drink orders, and I settled in for a night with a group of women who were a tight family unit. What I hadn't expected was that they would welcome me with open arms, and by the time Quin took me home, I felt like I'd found lifelong friends.

NINE

Lyric

I WAVED TO Quin, closed and locked my door and headed into my kitchen…just as my doorbell rang. I frowned. I made my way back and pulled open the door. "What did you forget?"

"Why the fuck are you opening the door without finding out who's on the other side?" Doom snapped.

I was so taken aback by the angry voice, I almost tripped over my boot, but his arm whipped out to steady me.

"What are you doing here?" I demanded, at the same time slapping at his arm holding me. When he didn't answer, I looked up and met his eyes. "Lincoln? Why are you here?"

"I came to apologize."

"Well, you're off to a stellar start. Let me go," I demanded, pulling my arm away.

He released me and let out a series of curses.

I closed the door and locked it, leaving him on the front porch. He knocked again, but I ignored him. My phone buzzed and I glanced at the screen and sighed. "What do you want, Lincoln?"

"I'm sorry, Angel. I really did come to apologize. You opening the door like that just freaked me out. You gotta be more vigilant."

"Careful, Doom, you're gonna start sounding like you care, and that's not the deal we made."

"I can't fuck you casually and care that you not get murdered at the same time?"

"Fine." I rolled my eyes. "I accept your apology."

"Thank you. Now, can I come in?"

"Are you gonna get pissed off and ghost me again?"

"I really didn't mean to ghost you." He sighed. "If you let me in, I'll explain."

I unlocked the door and pulled it open, stepping back to let him in. He followed me back to the kitchen and I sat at the island while he grabbed a beer from the fridge.

"Sure, Doom, help yourself."

"I bought it," he retorted.

"Oh, right."

I'd forgotten about that. He'd brought over a case the week before so I'd have it on hand. He'd also bought a couple bottles of my favorite red. Apparently, I'd blocked his kindness out.

"How was girls' night?" he asked.

"It was really fun. I explained in great detail the shape of your dick. They were enthralled."

"I suppose I deserve that," he said.

"And worse."

He came around to my side of the island and turned my stool so I was facing him, lifting my chin and stroking my cheek. "I was a dick, Lyric. I can't promise it won't happen again, but I'm tryin'."

"Try harder."

"Okay, Lyric, I'll try harder."

He leaned down to kiss me, but I covered his mouth with my fingers. "Why did you ghost me?"

"You know how there's shit you can't talk about because of attorney-client privilege?"

"Yes."

"Well, there's things I can't talk about because it's club business. There's shit going on right now that made it impossible for me to call, but I wanted to."

"What kinds of things?"

"I can't talk about it. It's club business."

I smiled. "But you wanted to."

"I did."

"Well, bless your heart," I crooned.

"Lyric—"

"No, Doom. This is all lip service." I sighed. "Look, I don't know who you think you're talking to, but I told you I don't want a commitment, so I don't need excuses. But I also will not be spoken to the way you did last week. You've apologized, I've accepted that apology. It's all good. But don't insult my intelligence and lie to me."

He dragged his hands through his hair. "You're right. I'm sorry. It's been a shit week."

"At the risk of irritating you more, I know it's been a shitty week, Doom, because none of the women have seen you."

"Fuck me."

"They're worried about you."

"So you told them... about us?"

"No!" I rushed to say. "I told you I wouldn't. You came up naturally in conversation. It was cute, actually, because they kept reminding me who you were when they brought you up. Like, Quin would say, 'Doom hasn't slept at the compound all week. Oh, Lyric, Doom is the guy your sister bid on.' If they had any inkling about us, they didn't let on."

He shook his head, looking like the weight of the world was on his shoulders. I reached out and grabbed his vest, tugging him toward me. "Hey, I've got your back. So do those women. I don't know what's going on with you, and if you don't want to disclose, I won't push you, but I'm here if you need me."

He relaxed a little. "Thanks, Angel."

"But seriously, don't lie to me. I'll end this faster than a knife fight in a phone booth."

"That's fair."

"Willow said something about you disappearing this time every year."

"Fuckin' Willow." He stiffened again and I squeezed his hand.

"Tell me."

"Jesus," he whispered. "My wife died."

"She did?"

He nodded. "With my son."

I bit back tears. "What happened?"

That's when his demeanor kind of... well, shut down.

"Drunk driver. I was on shift and got the call. We arrived on scene and the car was engulfed in flames. I got Ezra out, but Jennifer was DOA. Ezra died two days later. That was ten years ago. Tuesday was the anniversary."

"And it's why you quit being a firefighter?"

He nodded, but he was stilted. Almost like he wasn't in his body.

"Hey," I whispered, reaching up to stroke his face, but he reared back like I'd hit him.

"Fuck!" he bellowed.

He turned to walk away, but I reached for him again. "Wait. Doom, you can't leave like this. Just take a minute."

He tried to pull away again, but I held fast.

"Lincoln, I need you to look at me. I'll let you go, but I'm not letting you leave until I know you're okay."

He looked at me, but it took a little while for me to know that he saw me. Once his body unlocked, I relaxed and gave his arm a squeeze. "There you are."

"Sorry."

"Nothing to be sorry for." I smiled. "I'm assuming everyone knows. At the club?"

"No. Doc and Alamo know, so I assume they've told their women, but it's not common knowledge amongst the brothers. I don't know what the fuck Willow knows, though. She's like a voodoo witch who can read your soul or some shit just by look-ing at you."

I bit back a chuckle. "She's got that quiet cool thing going for sure."

"I don't think Quin knows, though. She keeps tryin' to set me up with her friends. It got so bad, I had to have Badger shut it down."

"Did he?"

He shrugged. "Haven't asked. As long as her harping stops…" He shook his head. "She needs to understand I'll never have that again. They all need to understand that."

"What about love? You don't want that again? More kids?"

"I'm gonna head out," he said without answering my ques-tions.

I could see he was calmer, so I nodded. "Okay. Thanks for coming by."

"I'll text you this week."

"Sounds good."

Then he was gone.

* * *

Doom

Saturday night, I headed downstairs, the pig roast in full swing. I got a few surprised looks, but no one said anything as I made my way into the kitchen for a beer.

"Hey, brother," Alamo said as I pulled open the refrigerator.

"Hey."

"You gonna hang?"

"Was thinkin' about it."

He smiled. "I like that, Doom."

A feminine gasp had me turning toward Jasmine and I rolled my eyes.

"I'm sorry, who are you?" she joked. "I don't think we've met."

I chuckled. "Good to see you too, babe."

She walked over to me and wrapped her arms around my waist. I didn't hug her back, not entirely sure what to do with my arms.

"Just go with it," Alamo instructed. "Once she locks on, she sticks. You should know that by now."

"Uncle Doom!" Kinsey, Badger and Quin's daughter, came bounding into the kitchen. "Will you come play pool with me? Dad's cheating."

I chuckled. "Sure."

Jasmine released me, but reached up and patted my cheek. "Really glad you're here, honey."

I nodded and followed Kinsey out to the great room and over to the pool table where Badger and Quin were deep in a game.

"What's this about you cheatin', Badger?"

Quin chuckled. "He's still losing."

"It's true," Badger admitted, leaning down nose-to-nose with his daughter. "But you seem to forget that snitches get stitches."

"And you seem to forget that I'm club business, so I'm always protected," Kinsey retorted.

He laughed. "Good girl."

For the next two hours, I communed with my brothers and their families. I hadn't felt this light in years and I knew it was because of Lyric. I tried not to put too much stock in that fact, but she was growing on me. Becoming important to me.

There was a freedom in knowing there was no pressure for anything more. No expectations. Maybe that was why I felt like the noose was loosening a little.

As midnight approached, I headed into the kitchen for another beer, walking in as Willow, Quin, and Olivia were putting food away, and overheard part of their conversation.

"Did you invite her tonight?" Willow asked.

"Lyric?" Quin asked.

My ears perked up.

"Yes."

"I did. But she had a date. Some guy named Wes. I'll give her more notice next time so she can make it. Oh, hey Doom."

"Hey," I said, grabbing a beer and walking out of the room and straight for the bar. I suddenly needed a bottle of tequila to go with my beer.

Fuck.

I snagged the Sauza and headed for my room.

"Doom?" Willow called.

Jesus, shit, fuck balls.

I turned to face her. "Hey, babe."

She cocked her head. "You okay?"

"Yep."

"Something changed."

"Will—"

She stepped closer. "Look, I know you keep your demons shoved deep inside. I've seen them," she whispered. "My heart breaks for you and what you've had to carry, but tonight, for a little while, anyway, something was different. And now it's not."

I closed my eyes briefly. How the fuck this woman knew how to get to the heart of me freaked me the fuck out.

"I had a dream," she continued.

I met her eyes and saw that tears were forming.

"Your family—"

"Stop," I rasped.

She nodded, tears slipping onto her cheeks. "You are loved Doom. Deeply. You're not alone. Please remember that."

I turned and rushed up to my room, closing and locking the door behind me in an effort to shut out the world.

* * *

"Vehicle on fire, Louisville Road, all units respond."

I suited up and followed my crew into the rig, heading to the fire just like I'd done a thousand times before.

Pulling up to the scene, my lieutenant and I made a run for the car, but I was suddenly intercepted and dragged away. "What the fuck?"

"Linc, you need to back off," Dustin, second lieutenant, ordered.

"What? Why?" I looked up and it hit me. It was Jennifer's car on fire. "Goddammit."

I pulled away from Dustin and made a run for the inferno. "Lincoln!"

I tried to pull the door open but it was fused shut. The win-

dow was open and Jennifer was groaning quietly. "Baby, I'm here. I'm gonna get you out."

"Get Ez," she rasped.

"My kid's in the back!" I bellowed, and my brothers moved in perfect unison as the flames continued to cover the car.

"Baby, I've got you."

"I love you, Lincoln."

"I love you, too, Jenny Bean. Stay awake for me. I got you. We're gettin' Ezra, okay? We've got a party to plan, so I need you to hold on."

I was forcibly removed from the car, despite my protests.

"You stay there, or I'm gonna chain you to the rig," Dustin warned. "Let them work."

They finally got Ezra out and loaded him into an ambulance. I chose to go with him while they continued to get Jennifer out. The fire had been contained, so I was confident she'd be okay.

I was wrong.

They rushed my boy to the burn unit and straight into surgery. I waited a few minutes, and then I went to find out about my wife, but when a doctor approached me, I just knew...

"Mr. Marxx, I'm very sorry. Your wife suffered a massive heart attack from the smoke inhalation. We were unable to save her or the baby."

"The baby?"

"She was pregnant. You didn't know?"

I collapsed to my knees...

I sat up with a growl, the bottle of tequila beside me on the bed. I lifted it and threw it against the wall. I let Lyric in, goddammit. What the fuck was wrong with me? I needed to shut this down. I would never allow myself to go through anything like that again.

Ever.

TEN

Lyric

Two weeks later...

I'D HAD ANOTHER date with Wes, but Doom had been busy, so I'd been denied some much needed relief. He'd texted and kept me updated this time, though, so he'd kept his promise.

I knew I was going to need to make a decision about next steps with Wes once the boot was off, he'd said as much, but until that happened, he was happy to enjoy my company without sex.

The more I got to know him, the more I liked him, but I honestly didn't know if he'd be around long-term. He probably wanted a family and I was not the woman to give him one, so I

81

should really cut my losses and move on, but I decided I'd wait until the subject came up.

This was what I was stewing on when my cell phone rang at four o'clock Friday afternoon. "Lyric Morgan."

"This is an automated courtesy call from Coastal State Prison to inform you that prisoner, 24961, Garrett Smalls has been released..."

I didn't hear the rest, mostly because I'd dropped my cell phone in shock.

Oh, God. No.

Knowing I couldn't really put coherent sentences together, I retrieved my phone from the floor and called my sister.

"Hi, LiLi."

"Garrett," I panted into the phone.

"Garrett Smalls?"

"Is out."

"Shit, okay, where are you?"

"At the office."

"Stay there until I call you back."

"Okay," I whispered.

"Let Leo know what's going on, but do *not* leave."

"I won't," I promised. I hung up and headed down to my boss's office. His door was open, but I still knocked before walking in.

Leo Walker's father had started the firm back in the sixties and Leo had taken it over and built it up to be one of the top firms in Savannah.

"Lyric? You look like you've seen a ghost. Sit down," Leo directed, and I lowered myself into a chair across from his desk.

"Garrett Smalls has been released," I said. "I just got the call."

"Wow. Do you know why? He was supposed to be in for life." He leaned against his desk and crossed his arms.

I shook my head. "No clue."

"I know this is bad timing, but you should probably hand everything on your plate off to Georgia and get out of town for a few days. At least until you can figure out what's going on."

"I have a feeling that's exactly what my sister's going to say.

She's looking into it now."

"Right, well, whatever you need, Lyric. You can work remotely, or not. You're in no risk of losing your partnership here."

I smiled. "Thanks, Leo. I really appreciate it. For the moment, Harmony wants me to stick around here, so I'll keep you posted on future steps."

"Sounds good."

I left his office and headed back to mine, wanting to talk to the only person I knew would make me feel truly safe, so I called Doom. I also wanted to let him know about my appointment to get my boot off next week.

"Hey," he answered.

"Hi. How are you?"

"Good. You need somethin'?" He sounded irritated.

"Um...no. I just wanted to let you know I might be heading out of town for a few days."

"I've been meaning to call you," he said.

"Oh?"

"Yeah. I think we should part ways," he said.

My stomach dropped and I wrapped my arm around my waist, the sting of tears starting in the back of my nose.

"Lyric, you still there?"

"Oh, um, yes. Sorry."

"You good?" he asked.

No, my heart is breaking. Why the hell is my heart breaking?

"Yes. That's fine. No harm, no foul," I said, trying to sound confident.

"Great. Have a nice life."

And then he was gone. I closed my office door, leaning against it and bursting into tears. I felt like my soul was being ripped from my body. My stomach roiled and I couldn't catch my breath. The last time I felt like this was when I found out I'd never have a child of my own.

No. I refused to go through this again.

Luckily, I didn't have time to wallow, as my sister called back and my life was suddenly set on an unexpected trajectory.

Within thirty-six hours, I was in Portland, safely ensconced in my sister's home, Booger at Quin's, and my home locked up and surveilled by local cops.

Jaxon had reached out to his friends in Savannah and they were doing a deep dive into Garrett from there while I was safely on the other side of the country. Once it was safe for me to go back, they'd let me know, but until then, I was on forced vacation.

* * *

Doom

My phone buzzed and I pulled it out to see Dalton Moore was calling. "Dalt? Are you home?"

Dalton lived part time in Scotland and part time here with his wife, Andi. He was supposedly ex-FBI, but he consulted a lot for them, so I got the impression he did more hours now as a consultant than when he was an agent.

"Yeah, brother, thought you might want to get a beer tonight."

"Sure, man."

"Okay, I'll text you the details."

"Sounds good." I hung up and pulled up the invoice spreadsheet I'd been trying to reconcile all afternoon. Without success.

I dragged a hand down my face.

Fuck.

I missed Lyric.

The narcissist in me kind of hoped she'd at least try to reach out once or twice, but she didn't. When she'd said, 'no harm, no foul,' she'd meant it.

I shouldn't be surprised. I was a temporary fling. She needed me like a fuckin' hole in the head and she'd probably turn to Wes the CEO going forward.

Fuck, that thought made me crazy.

With my brain unable to focus on anything useful, I decided to close up shop early and head out. This was the beauty of having a non-walk-in clientele… I made my own hours.

"Rabbit, I'm closin' early. Lock up."

"Okay, brother. 'Night."

I passed by the customer service area and the news was on, a familiar face came on the screen and my blood ran cold. I grabbed the remote and turned the sound up.

"Garrett Smalls has been released on a technicality, but according..."

"Fuck," I snapped, shutting off the TV and making a run for my bike and heading straight for Lyric's.

It looked like it was locked up tight. I banged on her door, but no answer, so I sent her a text, then made my way to the compound. Jesus, if he was out, I wanted her guarded.

I walked in and froze.

"Why the fuck do you have Lyric's cat?"

Quin frowned. "How did you know this was Lyric's cat?"

"Where's Lyric?"

My phone buzzed before Quin could answer and I pulled it out to see a text from Lyric.

Out of town for a few days. Everything's fine. Quin's watching Booger.

"You know Lyric?" Quin asked.

"It looks like Doom knows Lyric very well," Olivia piped in. "Biblically speaking, even."

"Jesus," I hissed.

"Exactly," Olivia retorted.

"That's why," Willow said, and even though no one else had any idea what she was talking about, I did.

I shook my head, turned on my heel, and walked back out the door.

* * *

Lyric

Where are you? Why the fuck aren't you home?

Well, so much for 'have a nice life.' God, I was so over his alpha male bullshit. I texted him back, because I was polite, then turned off my phone and headed downstairs to see what I could make for dinner.

Harmony was in her office going through a suspect's books trying to find the smoking gun in his accounting records. She'd been at it for three days while Jaxon worked on my case from the FBI office downtown.

"I found it!" Harmony squeaked, and came out of her office doing a little dance. "I found the missing money, I found the missing money. The bastard's going do-ow-own," she sang.

I giggled, then everything went black.

"…I don't know, Jax, she went down. Hard. Yes, I've called 9-1-1."

"What happened?" I rasped and tried to sit up.

"Don't move," Harmony ordered. "I've called an ambulance.

"I'm fine."

"Jax, I'll call you back." She hung up and leaned over me. "Don't move, LiLi. You might have a clot. We need to get you to the hospital."

"God, I'm so sick of this boot."

"I know, honey. It comes off in three hours."

"Well, maybe not now."

The ambulance arrived within six minutes and I was loaded into it and driven to the hospital, where I was poked and prodded and left to stare at a semi-white wall while they interpreted the tests.

Harmony had called Cassidy who'd promptly come over and taken care of the kids, then came with me in the ambo.

"I think this is total overkill," I said, with a sigh.

"Humor me," Harmony said, staring at the magazine she'd been flipping through for an hour.

"I heard someone decided to play damsel in distress and faint."

I looked up and smiled. Macey Stone walked in and gave me a hug. She was married to Dallas, one of Jaxon's FBI partners and was a nurse, apparently a nurse at this hospital.

"Hi, Macey," I said.

Harmony stood and hugged her. "Are you here to cut through the red tape?"

She chuckled. "If I can. I'm going to see if I can get Alec on it."

"Okay, Mace, thanks," Harmony said.

I'd met Alec Stone once. He was Dallas's brother and a doctor. Head of ER, if I remembered correctly, so he was a good person to know.

Fifteen minutes later, he walked in with Macey behind him.

"Hi Lyric, it's good to see you again."

I smiled. "You too. Can you please tell my sister I don't have a blood clot?"

"Lyric does not have a blood clot." He turned back to me. "But...you do have a baby."

"Right." I laughed, sitting up. "Cute. Okay. So, why did I faint?"

"You're pregnant."

I felt the prick of tears and looked at Harmony, begging silently for help. She jumped up from her seat and grabbed my hand. "No, Alec, there must be some mistake."

He pulled the chart up on the monitor. "The bloodwork clearly shows a high level of the pregnancy hormone. I'd like to do a vaginal ultrasound just to be—"

"No," I said, swallowing convulsively. "You don't understand. NiNi, *help.*"

"Alec, she was stabbed. Twelve years ago. The doctors said her uterus was damaged beyond repair and she'd never be able to conceive, let alone carry a child. This just isn't possible."

"Let's do this," he said. "Let's do a quick vaginal ultrasound. If I don't see anything, then we'll figure out what else is going on."

"Is that okay, LiLi?" Harmony asked me, and I nodded, but I honestly wasn't sure what I was agreeing too, I was in so much shock.

"Okay, I'll let you get changed and Macey'll prep the room. I'll be back in a few."

Alec left and I moved in robot fashion, Harmony directing while Macey got the room ready.

There was no way. None.

Alec returned and pulled a chair up beside me. "Ready?"

I nodded and he slid the probe into me, the image popping onto the screen and I squinted in an effort to figure out what I was seeing.

Alec smiled. "That's a baby."

I gripped my sister's hand like a talisman and burst into silent tears as he pointed to the screen. "I'm picking up a definite heartbeat. I'd guess you're about six weeks along."

I did the math and realized I'd gotten pregnant the first night I was with Doom.

Oh my god. I'm having the baby of a man who wants nothing to do with either one of us.

* * *

Doom

I walked into the restaurant where I was meeting Dalton, and headed to the bar. He was on his phone, but gave me a chin lift and waved to the stool next to him.

"No way. Jesus, is she okay? Okay, yeah, no problem. We're working on it. You got it. Okay, Jax. Talk to you soon, bye."

"Everything okay?"

Dalton nodded. "Yeah. Jaxon's sister-in-law was rushed to emergency."

"Melody?" I asked hopefully.

"Have you met Melody?"

"I have," I said, starting to relax. "I've met all three sisters, actually."

"Oh. No, actually, it was Lyric. I think she's fine. But Harmony was freaked."

Fuck, fuck, fuck.

"I can imagine."

The bartender walked over, giving me a moment with my thoughts while Dalton ordered a beer. I ordered the same, then tried to make small talk, all the while trying not to look like I was worrying about a woman I wasn't supposed to care about.

Thankfully, Dalton got called away, cutting our night short, so I headed back to the compound and up to my room to pack a bag. Before I could even make it to the stairs, however, Willow called my name.

Goddammit.

"Will—"

"Before you say anything," she said, interrupting me. "I

booked you a flight to Portland."

"Come again?"

"I emailed you the confirmation number and itinerary. It leaves at six a.m. tomorrow."

"Will—"

She raised her hand and cut me off again. "I know you don't want anyone to know about Lyric. I won't say a word, but you care about her and you've obviously done something really stupid. This is your chance to make it right."

"Jesus, woman, why the hell aren't you afraid of me?"

"Why would I be?" She smiled. "You try to show a hard outer shell, but anyone willing to see you, knows you're all squishy inside."

I reached out and pulled her against me, hugging her tightly. "Fuck, Willow. You scare the shit out of me."

She hugged me back. "I know, Doom. It's because I can see your squishy bits."

I released her, cupping her face. "Does Dash know how lucky he is?"

"Absolutely."

"Thanks, sweetheart."

"Anytime, buddy. Seriously."

She turned to walk away, but I called her name. "How did you know about my family?"

"I had a dream. I don't know all the details, but I know you lost them." She gave me a sad smile. "I'm really sorry, Doom."

I gave her a chin lift, then headed upstairs.

ELEVEN

Lyric

I SLEPT IN on Saturday, unusual for me, but I think I was still in quite a bit of shock. It might have been because I'd had my boot removed yesterday, so nothing was tugging at me. It was total freedom and I loved it.

"Shh, Sky, let Aunty sleep," Harmony whispered outside my door.

"But she never sleeps this late."

"Move away from Aunty's door, Peanut," Jaxon added, and then all was quiet.

I slid my hand to my stomach and closed my eyes again.

A baby.

It was almost too much to hope for.

"I don't know if you're real, Lil' Blip, but if you are, I'm going to love you so, so much. I promise," I whispered.

I took a deep breath and forced myself out of my cocoon of fantasy, taking a quick shower and walking gingerly downstairs where Skyler wrapped me in a bear hug. I still had to be careful, wear flats for at least six months, and avoid being on my feet for too long.

"Careful of your Aunty," Harmony warned.

"I'm okay," I said, and hugged Skyler back. "I'm always up for hugs from my Sky."

Jaxon and Ares walked in a few minutes later, and Ares set his baseball cap on the island.

"No practice, huh?" Harmony asked.

"Rained out," Jaxon said, kissing her gently, then kissing my cheek. "How are you feeling?"

"I'm good, Jax. Thanks."

"Cap in the mudroom, buddy," Jaxon instructed and Ares obeyed immediately. "Who wants waffles?"

"Me," three feminine voices resounded, along with a little boy voice.

Jaxon grinned and pulled the waffle iron out of the cabinet.

Harmony pulled me off the stool I was sitting on and guided me into the front room. It was sort of private and I could tell she wanted to talk.

We sat facing each other on her fancy sofa and I smiled. "What's up?"

"So, what's the plan?"

I chuckled. "I don't have a plan. I'm still not convinced any of this is real."

"Have you told Wes?"

"Wes?"

"Hello, the guy you've been dating?"

Oh, shit, Wes.

I bit my lip. "Um, Wes isn't the father. We haven't even slept together."

"What. The. Hell?" Harmony squeaked.

"Mom? Are you okay?" Skyler came rushing into the room, sitting in between us, and handing her a jar with money. "You said hell, you need to put a dollar in."

"Yeah, baby, we're fine," Harmony said, pulling a dollar from her sweats pocket and dropping it in. "Aunty was just telling me something surprising."

"Oh, what was it?"

"Sky!" Jaxon called. "Come help with the waffles."

Skyler wrinkled her nose, but did what her father told her.

"Who's the father?" Harmony whispered.

I dropped my head in my hands and shook my head. "It doesn't really matter. He wants nothing to do with me, so he's not going to want anything to do with the baby."

"Oh, honey, I'm sorry."

"It's fine," I lied as I burst into tears.

"Oh, LiLi, what happened?" she asked, wrapping an arm around me.

"I have no idea! It was all supposed to be really casual and that was *my* rule. It was good. But then I fell in love with him and I didn't realize it until the second he called to say he didn't want our arrangement to continue."

She kissed my temple and sighed. "I'm sorry, honey."

"It's fine. He's been very clear from the beginning that he has no interest in having kids and I refuse to be a liar."

"But you're not a liar."

"I know, but he won't see it that way. He'll see it as me trapping him into something he didn't want." I pulled away from my sister. "It's fine. He doesn't need to know. The odds of this pregnancy actually lasting is a crapshoot, so there's no point in saying anything anyway."

"Who, LiLi?"

"I will tell you, but I swear to God, if you tell anyone—"

"I would never."

"Even Jaxon."

She bit her lip. "I can't keep it from Jax, honey."

"Then I can't tell you," I whispered.

"Honey, just give it up. Jaxon won't tell anyone. You know he won't."

"Doom."

"Holy fucking shit!"

Skyler appeared with the jar again and thrust it toward Harmony. "Ten dollars. You said two of the bad ones."

"I think we need to get your hearing tested for supersonic abilities."

"You did kind of yell, sweetness," I pointed out.

"I don't have my wallet. Tell Dad I'll owe him."

"Did Aunty tell you something else surprising?"

Harmony smiled at Skyler. "Honey child, I love you. I love how inquisitive you are, but right now, what you're doing is bordering on nosy, which is rude. Aunty and I are having an adult conversation that contains subject matter that isn't appropriate for you, but I promise, you're not missing out on anything, and we'll have time together, just the three of us where we'll be able to talk about whatever you want. For the moment, though, you need to go hang with Ares and Daddy in the kitchen and not interrupt us again. If you do, you're going to lose some privileges. Understand?"

"Yes, Mama," she said, and walked out of the room.

"Good job, Mama," I said.

"I'm trying to beat the precociousness out of her without breaking her spirit," Harmony admitted. "God, I hate precocious children. They give me the creeps."

I chuckled. "Remember Melody at that age?"

"Why do you think I want to raise a confident girl who isn't creepy?"

"You're doing an amazing job, NiNi."

"Thanks, honey." Harmony smiled. "Now, tell me about Doom."

"He and Alamo were the ones who kind of rescued me after the accident and Doom pulled all of my stuff out of my car and brought it to me at the hospital. It was really kind. I can't imagine where my laptop, purse, and case notes might have ended up if left in the hands of some random tow truck driver."

"Seriously."

"We kind of kept bumping into each other, and I made the mistake of telling him I ran that background check on him, which really pissed him off."

"Jaxon told you," Harmony said.

"I know." I sighed. "I found out where his compound was

and took everything I had down there. I still have no idea what Shawn found. I gave it to Doom and apologized and he fucked me quite thoroughly, boot and all."

"Oh, my."

"Yes. Oh, my indeed." I licked my lips, the memory coming back and making me want him all over again. "That's the night I got pregnant, I think."

"What about Wes?"

I shrugged. "We've gone out on a few dates, but he says he doesn't want to rush things in the sex department. He said he was willing to wait for the boot to come off."

"Which is sweet and gentlemanly, but you're not really looking for a gentleman, right?"

"Not after having Doom, no, not really. Doom got creative."

"I get it."

"But he's had some really bad breaks, Harmony, so I'm not going to add to his trauma. If this baby is for real and if I can bring this pregnancy to term, I will raise him or her the best I can, but I'll have to do it without Doom." I leaned over and squeezed her arm. "You cannot tell Jaxon's family, NiNi. Promise me. If Aidan or Carter let it slip, Doom will feel obligated to do the right thing, and I will not start a relationship like that."

"Okay, honey, I promise."

"Thanks."

"Waffles!" Jaxon called, and we headed into the kitchen.

* * *

Doom

The plane touched down just after ten a.m. Portland time, and I was dog tired, but all I wanted to do was get my arms around Lyric and apologize. I figured I should probably wash the stink of plane and desperation off me first, so I headed toward the taxis.

I ran into Hatch on the way, however. Hatch Wallace was the newly patched president of the Portland chapter of the Dogs of Fire, having been the Sgt. at Arms before that. He was as OG as it got, and he was respected by every one of us.

He smiled as I approached. "I'm the welcoming committee."

"Thanks, man. You didn't need to come out."

"You feel free to tell Maisie that. I'll take you to the compound where you can clean up, but Maisie has asked that you join us for dinner at least one night while you're here."

I grinned. "I'd be honored."

"That is the correct answer."

I chuckled and followed him to his truck.

"How'd you know I was comin'?" I asked as we drove.

"Willow called Maisie."

"'Course she did."

"You wanna fill me in?"

"Not really."

"Is your shit gonna bleed into the club?" Hatch asked.

"No."

"Well, if that changes, I'm gonna need you to divulge, but otherwise, whatever you need, consider the club your home while you're here."

"Thanks, Hatch."

"We got a family night tonight. It'd be good if you join."

That wasn't really a request, so I nodded. "I'll be there."

"Good."

The Portland compound was located behind Ernie's Auto Body and it was like a fortress. He led me through a couple of doors and a foyer before we entered a large great room with pool tables, sofas, a TV, and chairs.

"Darling, is that you?"

I recognized Maisie's sweet, British voice calling from the kitchen. I'd met her the few times she'd accompanied Hatch to visit Savannah.

"Yeah, Sunshine."

She walked out of the kitchen and smiled. "Hi, Doom."

"Hey, Maisie."

She opened her arms.

"I stink like plane," I warned.

"I don't care," she said, wrapping me in a hug. "How are you, love?"

"I'm good, thanks."

Hatch grabbed a key from a drawer and handed it to me. "Top of the stairs, second door on the right."

"Thanks, brother."

"There's fresh bread and lunch meat, so if you'd like a sandwich, let me know and I'll be happy to make you something," Maisie offered.

"Thanks, Maisie, I'm good," I said. "I'm gonna go take a shower."

"Okay, love."

I headed upstairs and closed myself in the room, pulling out my cell phone and calling Lyric. It went to voicemail.

"Angel, will you call me when you get this? Just want to make sure you're okay."

* * *

Lyric

"Angel, will you call me when you get this? Just want to make sure you're okay."

"I think you've lost your ever-blessed mind," I whispered out loud.

Angel?

Um, no.

Will you call me when you get this?

Again, no.

I grabbed my bag and joined my family in the kitchen where we were communing before heading up to the Dogs of Fire club for a family night. I, for one, was looking forward to good food and loud music. I needed a distraction.

"Okay, family, in the car," Harmony directed, and the kids made a run for the garage.

"They're almost as excited as I am," I said with a laugh.

"Oh my god, they love family nights. And I love that I can drink whatever I want and Jaxon is the designated driver."

"Well, tonight I can do that if he wants to drink."

She grinned. "That's true, huh?"

We headed into the garage and climbed into the car, then Jaxon drove us out to the club, arriving to find the parking lot filled with more bikes than you'd see at a Harley dealership, along with a few other vehicles as well.

As soon as the kids were released from their booster seats, they made a run for the doors and were inside before we'd even hit the threshold. Jaxon jogged after them and Harmony and I followed with the desserts and wine we'd brought.

We headed into the kitchen, finding Maisie inside with her daughter, Poppy, laughing about something, but when they saw us, they rushed to help.

"I didn't realize you were coming as well," Poppy said, hugging me. "I'm so glad."

I'd met the entire Portland club last Christmas when Melody and I'd come for their Christmas fundraiser. It was a blast and I planned to join them every year I could.

"Surprise," I said with a laugh.

"Now I get it," Maisie said, hugging me as well.

"You get what?" I asked.

"You're here."

"Yes. I'm here… to see Harmony."

"No. I mean you're here, so he's here."

"I'm sorry, Maisie, I'm not tracking," I admitted.

She pulled away and smiled. "You don't know?"

"I don't know what?"

"Darling, Doom's here."

"What?" I rasped.

"What do you mean, he's here?" Harmony demanded.

"He flew in this morning," Maisie said.

"What?" I squeaked. "Why?"

"For you, obviously," Maisie said.

"I need to go," I whispered, turning to my sister. "I need to go."

"Okay, honey. I'll get the keys and take you home."

I shook my head. "No, I'll Uber. It's okay. Just get me out of here."

"Too late, love," Maisie said, and I saw Doom walk in with Hatch.

God, he looked wrecked.

Good. He should.

"Hey," he said.

"I was just leaving," I said. "Sorry, Maisie."

"I'll get the keys," Harmony repeated.

I shook my head. "You stay. I'll grab an Uber."

"You're not goin' anywhere alone, Lyric."

This came from Doom, and it was almost my undoing.

Almost.

"I'm going to kill him, NiNi," I hiss-pered. "Not a hair, not a fiber."

"You probably shouldn't say that in front of me." Harmony smiled gently. "FBI and all."

I scowled. "I don't plan on leaving any witnesses."

Harmony laughed. "Give me two minutes and I'll get—"

"I will take you home, but not until after we talk," Doom said, cutting off my sister.

I glared at him. "Don't interrupt my sister when she's being ridiculous."

"I apologize, Harmony." He crossed his big, beefy arms. "I'd like to borrow your sister for a few minutes."

Harmony looked at me. "It's up to you, LiLi."

I stared at my sister, keeping my back to Doom. "I don't know if I can," I whispered.

"Sweetness, you'll never know if you don't try."

I nodded and turned to face Doom again. "Five minutes."

He held his hand out to me, but I refused to touch him as I followed him out of the kitchen, down a hall and upstairs. He opened a door at the top of the stairs and stepped back so I could precede him in, flipping the light on as I walked inside.

"You got your boot off," he said.

I nodded. "Yesterday."

"You hurtin'?"

"Not so far." I faced him. "But I don't think you want to waste your five minutes on discussing my boot, do you?"

"Jesus, I was an ass."

I sighed. "No you weren't."

"How do you figure?"

"You were just sticking with the terms of our agreement, Doom," I said. "I didn't fault you for that."

"Yeah, but I did."

"Why?" I asked.

"Because I'm in love with you."

"No."

"Yes. I should have told you sooner, but on top of being an ass, I'm stubborn as all get out—"

"Oh my god. Stop," I hissed, heading for the door. I almost tripped on my skirt. Because I'd been forced to pack quickly, I'd packed my trusty maxi skirts that accommodated my boot, which were now a tad long with just flipflops on.

He grabbed my arm gently and pulled me back to him. "Angel, I need to say this."

I burst into tears and tore my arm from him. "Don't touch me!"

"Jesus, what the hell's wrong?"

I waved my hands in front of my face, as I was in serious danger of hyperventilating. "Oh, god."

"Baby, what the fuck?" he whispered, closing the distance between us.

He reached out to me but didn't touch me. Just waited for me to come to him.

"You don't und...er...stand," I sobbed. "I'm so...sor... sor...sorry."

"Lyric, I know you were with that Wes guy. I don't care about—"

"No!" I growled, trying to wipe my face as I took a deep breath.

"Jesus, you need to sit down before you pass out," he said, inching toward me.

"I need to go."

"You're not goin' anywhere until we work this out."

I shook my head. "I need to go."

He wrapped his arms around me and I tried to push away but he held tight. "Baby, talk to me."

I couldn't breathe, let alone talk.

He lifted me, carrying me to the chair against the window, sitting down and settling me in his lap. "It's okay, Angel, I've got you."

I had no fight left in me. I laid my head on his shoulder pressed my face into his neck, crying for everything I'd lost, then gained, and what I was about to lose again. I was sure the second he found out I was pregnant with a baby that probably wouldn't make it to term, he'd freak and run again. And I just knew it would break me, so I took what he offered for the moment, hoping it would be a memory I could pull from when I needed it.

It took several minutes for the hiccups and sobbing to calm, and Doom held me, stroking my hair as I gripped his vest and took in his essence.

"You're okay," he whispered. "You can tell me anything."

"Not this, I can't."

"Baby, you can." I tried to push off his lap, but he held firm. "Settle."

"Doom, you're not going to like what I have to tell you."

"You're still stayin' right here while you say it."

"I'm pregnant."

TWELVE

Doom

I WAS SURE I'd heard her wrong. "Come again?"

"I'm pregnant. With your baby," she added in a rush. "I have no idea how it happened. It probably won't make it to term, but it's still a miracle. Somehow my uterus healed itself, and now it's cradling our baby. But it's a hope I'm scared to death to believe in, because I'm probably going to get my heart ripped out of my chest."

"What?" I rasped, my heart in my throat.

She made a lame attempt to push at my shoulders. "Can I get up now?"

"No." I held her tighter. "Tell me everything."

"I was scheduled to go in and have the boot removed, but I passed out before my appointment, so they rushed me to the emergency room. When they ran tests and took X-rays to check for blood clots and whatnot, they discovered I was pregnant. I didn't believe them, so Alec insisted on a vaginal ultrasound—"

"Who's Alec?"

"Dr. Stone. You know Jaxon's partner, Dallas?"

I nodded. I knew *of* him, sort of.

"His brother." She frowned. "Can I finish now? *Without* you derailing me."

"Sorry, yes."

"Alec did the ultrasound, and, well, sure enough, there's a little blip in there," she said, running her hand over her belly. "But I have to see my OB because it's not supposed to be possible, which means it probably isn't and I'm probably going to lose the baby. I didn't want you to know because I don't want you to lose another child—"

Jesus, I couldn't watch her beautiful mouth form words anymore. I had to taste her. I pulled her head down and covered her mouth with mine, cutting off her worries.

She pushed away, breaking the kiss. "Don't, Lincoln. You're just making it harder to walk away."

"Who's walking away?"

"I'm assuming you are," she rasped.

"Oh, I'm not goin' anywhere. Neither are you."

"What?" she whispered.

"I love you."

"What?" she whispered again.

"I've been angry for a long fuckin' time and it's time I pull my head outta my ass and come into the light, don't you think?" I stroked her cheek, needing to feel the softness of her skin. "I have a second chance. One that is seemingly a miracle for both of us, and I'm gonna take it. Are you with me?"

"What if the baby...?" she didn't finish the thought and I was grateful for that.

"Nothing's gonna happen to the baby, honey. But, whatever happens, we'll face it together." I smiled. "I can do this if you're with me."

"You won't leave me?"

God, she was cute. Her nose and cheeks were red, but her light blue eyes were bright and all I saw was unconditional love staring back at me. The thought of ever being separated from her again gutted me. "I won't leave you."

She gripped my chin. "I'm serious, Lincoln. If you try to walk away, I will end you. No one will find anything. Not a hair, not a fiber…no marrow, no nothing."

I grinned. "I'm not goin' anywhere."

She kissed me, smiling against my lips. "By the way, I was never with Wes."

My heart raced. "No?"

She shook her head. "He didn't want to deal with my boot."

"Pussy."

She let out a quiet snort. "Well, he certainly missed out on mine, yes." Snuggling close again, she whispered, "I would have never slept with him."

"You don't think so?"

"No. I appreciate a man who's willing to get creative. Case in point, I fell in love with you the second you propped my stupid leg up on pillows, and then, when you dumped me, it was confirmed."

I cocked my head. "When I dumped you?"

"Well, it was actually right before it. When I found out Garrett was out, and all I wanted to do was call you because I knew you'd keep me safe."

"Shit, Angel, I'm sorry."

"You should be."

There she was. I smiled. "I was gonna keep you safe, Lyric."

"I figured. But it's not the same."

I stroked her back. "Safe's safe."

"Safe by the man you love who doesn't love you back, is not nearly as good as safe by the man you love who loves you back."

I kissed her nose. "You've got a point."

"Who's watching your shop?"

"Rabbit and Alamo."

"How long can you stay?"

"At least a week." I slid a lock of her hair behind her ear. "I'm not leavin' without you, though, so we'll need to work that out."

"Jaxon and Harmony want me here until the Garrett thing is sorted."

"The Garrett thing could take a while, so we need to figure out an alternative that keeps you safe, but keeps you with me."

She raised an eyebrow. "What do you propose?"

"Haven't gotten that far yet," I confessed. "You wouldn't be willing to live at the compound until he's behind bars or dead would you?"

She rolled her eyes. "No. If I'm not in my own home, then I want to be here with my sister. I don't get to see her and the kids nearly enough as it is."

"What about Booger?"

"Booger's a cat, he's happy eating dead things. Besides, he's being well cared for and you know it."

I sighed. "What about me?"

She smiled. "Am I, or am I not, sitting in your lap right now?"

"Yeah, but you're not on my dick, are you?"

Her nostrils flared and her mouth parted as she gasped quietly. "Let me fix that."

"You do that, Angel."

Kicking her flipflops off, she lifted her skirt and straddled me, her heat pressing against my already hard cock, and kissed me deeply. Staring down at me, she stroked my beard. "I love you, Lincoln."

"Love you, too, Lyric."

"I want you to do me a favor," she whispered.

"Anything."

"I want you to fuck me super dirty." Slipping her thumb into my mouth, she smiled. "From behind."

Jesus, I didn't think my dick could get any harder, but it did. I wrapped my arms around her and stood, kissing her again. She hooked her legs around my waist as I carried her to the bed and dropped her gently onto the mattress.

Before I could get her clothes off, however, someone banged on the door, and I had a feeling I knew exactly who it was.

"It's probably Harmony," Lyric said, sliding off the bed. "Give me a sec."

* * *

Lyric

I inched open the door and smiled at my sister. "Everything's okay."

"I figured." She handed me my purse. "Should I assume Doom will be bringing you home?"

"She's not comin' home tonight," he countered.

"Hey, you haven't groveled enough to make that statement, mister," I bossed.

"Did you tell him?" she whispered.

I smiled and nodded. "It's all really good, NiNi."

"I can't wait to hear about it. Will I see you before we leave?"

"Of course. We'll be down in a bit."

"An hour," Doom countered, and I blushed. "At least."

"I'll see you down there," Harmony said, and I closed and locked the door.

"You think you can last an hour?" I challenged, removing my T-shirt, then slipping out of my skirt.

He knelt in front of me, pressing his lips gently against my belly. "Hey, baby. Daddy here. I need you to look away now. I'm going to do some really nasty things to Mommy, and it might scar you for life."

I giggled, even as tears filled my eyes. I slid my fingers into his hair and he smiled up at me. "We're gonna have more," he avowed.

I nodded, suddenly unable to speak.

"Twelve."

I chuckled. "Let's see if I can get this one to stick, okay?"

"*We*, baby. Let's see if *we* can get this one to stick. You need to remember we're in this together."

"I'm thirty-six, honey, we're gonna have to get to gettin' if you want twelve."

He rose to his feet. "Are you willing to try for three?"

I slid his vest off his shoulders. "Yep."

"Four?"

105

I lifted his T-shirt and ran my tongue over his Dogs tattoo. "Sure."

"Are you trying to distract me from talking about making babies?"

"By getting you in the mood to do the thing that makes them? After you've already made one?" I pushed his T-shirt up and off his head. "Sure, we'll go with that."

He chuckled, kicking off his boots, then kissing me again as he slid my bra straps down my arms. "Your tits are bigger."

"There's no way you'd notice that after a week."

"I notice everything, Lyric," he countered, unsnapping my bra and dropping it on the floor. Slipping his hand under the waistband of my panties and between my legs, he smiled. "Soaked."

"So, you gonna make me wait through foreplay?"

He raised an eyebrow and tore my panties from my hips, and I couldn't stop a quiet squeak. "What am I going to put back on?"

"Nothing," he growled. "I'm gonna have full access to you all night."

I bit my lip. "I can get behind that."

"And now, I'm gonna get behind you. Lean over the chair."

I shivered, stepping over to the chair and leaning over it while he removed his jeans and walked toward me slowly. He kicked my feet apart gently, sliding a finger through my wetness, then he pushed two inside of me. I dropped my head back with a whimper. I wanted his dick, not his fingers.

As his digits swept my walls, his other hand ran down my spine, whisper soft. "Patience, Angel."

I groaned in frustration. "Doom."

"You gonna ask nice like?"

"Please?"

Then he was inside of me and I was being fucked royally, my ass in the air as I anchored myself to the chair.

"Yes, honey, yes," I hissed. "Harder."

He complied, burying himself deeper, then faster and faster until I screamed his name, my body locking and walls contracting around him as his dick pulsed inside of me. He pulled out of me, helping me stand, then lifting me onto the bed, and stretching out beside me. Holding me close, he kissed me and ran his fingers over my hip. "Jesus Christ, I've missed you, Angel."

"Well, that doesn't surprise me. I'm pretty fucking amazing. I leave a big void when I'm not there."

He laughed, giving me a gentle squeeze. "Yeah. I won't let you out of my sight again."

"Smart man." I kissed his chest. "How did Maisie know you were here for me?"

"I'm guessin' Willow."

"Really?"

He filled me in on his conversation with her and I couldn't stop the tears from forming again. "Oh my god, that's so sweet."

"Jesus, are you okay?"

"No," I sniffed. "Hormones totally suck."

"Jen was like th—" He stopped mid-sentence and shook his head.

I sat up so I could see his face. "Don't hide, Lincoln. Don't hide them."

He met my eyes and nodded, taking a few deep breaths.

"Do you want to tell me about them?" I asked.

"Yes, but not tonight."

"Okay, honey." I kissed him. "I'm so proud of you."

"Why?"

"Because you said her name and didn't shut down."

"That's all you, Angel," he said, stroking my cheek. "You calm me."

"I already know something about her."

"Oh yeah?"

I nodded. "She was a genius."

"How do you figure?"

"She locked onto you and didn't let go." I kissed him again. "I plan to do the same."

He rolled me onto my back and smiled. "I'm gonna make sure you never want to let go."

"I'm going to hold you to that."

Kissing me one more time, we got dressed and headed downstairs to join our family and friends.

We stepped into the great room and my stomach roiled. "Doom?"

"Yeah?"

I reached for his arm.

"Baby?"

"Sick."

I had to give him credit. He had a plastic bag under my chin faster than I could turn back toward the stairs, and I puked as daintily as I could, considering I was in a building full of people.

While I kept the bag under my face, he wrapped an arm around my waist and guided me down the hall and into the bathroom, closing us in and taking the bag from me. I knelt in front of the toilet and he took care of the bag before washing his hands, then sweeping my hair back and tying it with a band he kept on his wrist for his own hair.

"Give me three seconds," he said, and stepped out. I heard him bellow for my sister and then he was back with me and leaning against the sink. "I'm not gonna crowd you, baby, but you tell me what you need. I'll be right here."

I nodded and closed my eyes. I was exhausted all of a sudden.

A knock at the door brought my sister with saltines and pop, and once I felt like I could stand, I washed my hands and rinsed my mouth out, but I was still exhausted.

"Bed," Doom ordered.

"I have nothing with me," I countered.

"You don't need anything," he said. "I'll run out and pick up whatever you need tomorrow. But for now, you're gonna rest."

His tone left no room for argument, and I was way too tired anyway, so I nodded and let him lead me back upstairs.

Harmony followed with the Sprite and crackers, then hugged me and closed me in with my man.

THIRTEEN

Lyric

DOOM'S BEARD TICKLED me as he kissed my shoulder, sliding his hand to my belly. "How are you feeling?"

"As long as I don't move, I'm good," I said. "I think. What time is it?"

"Ten."

"Why am I so tired?" I complained.

I'd thrown up a few more times last night, but then I fell asleep and pretty much slept like the dead. I woke up a few minutes ago, which meant I'd had almost eleven hours of sleep, so the fact I still felt like I'd been hit by a truck was annoying as hell.

"Because you're growing a life inside of you." He kissed my shoulder again. "But today, you're staying where you are."

"Are you staying with me?"

I felt the bed dip as he climbed off the mattress. "Yeah, Angel. I'm gonna head downstairs and grab food, then I'll be back up."

I closed my eyes and snuggled into the pillow. "Okay."

"Hey."

I opened my eyes to find him leaning over me. "Hey."

"Love you."

I smiled. "Love you."

He kissed my forehead, then left me to sleep.

* * *

Doom

I was pretty sure Lyric fell back to sleep before I'd even closed the door. I headed downstairs and found Hatch in the kitchen making coffee. "Mornin'," he said.

"Hey."

"How's Lyric?"

I smiled. "Asleep."

He grinned. "Maisie too."

My phone buzzed in my pocket and I excused myself and walked into the great room. It was Alamo calling. "Hey, brother."

"Hey. Garrett Smalls was arrested."

"No shit?"

"He murdered a woman last night."

"Jesus Christ," I hissed. "What happened?"

"I don't know the details. It was on the news this morning, so I called Dalton. Garrett was caught in the act, which guarantees there's no way in hell he'll get off on a technicality now. It's good news for Lyric."

I let out a deep breath of relief. "Fucked up for the woman's poor family."

"Yeah," he agreed. "Our women will see if they can help. You get shit sorted with Lyric?"

I smiled. "She made me work for it, but yes."

Alamo chuckled. "Good for her."

"I'll check in with Jaxon and we'll figure out flights."

110

"Sounds good. If you need a few days, the shop's good on this end. Rabbit's got it handled."

"I appreciate that. I'll keep you posted."

"Thanks, brother."

We hung up and I made my way back into the kitchen. Hatch was gone, so I made coffee and breakfast, finding a tray and loading it up.

Heading upstairs, I walked in and set everything on the bureau just as Lyric walked out of the bathroom. She'd found one of my T-shirts and covered her previously naked body while I was downstairs, which I wasn't overly happy with.

"What?" she asked.

"Like you better naked, Angel."

She grinned. "Well, I was freezing. I'm not used to Portland and its bi-polar weather."

"Southern to the core."

"Damn straight."

I grinned. "You hungry?"

"Starved."

"Good. You eat while I fill you in on my news."

"You have news?" She grabbed a piece of toast and took a bite.

"Garrett's been arrested."

"Really?"

"He killed another woman."

"Oh my god, no." She set her toast down and shook her head. "Why wasn't he being watched?"

"I don't know any details, Angel. Alamo just called to say it was safe to come home."

"But it's all just so…clean. Easy."

"Not for the woman who got murdered."

"That's not what I mean." She shook her head. "This isn't how Garrett works. I need more information. Who was the woman who was killed? Was she random? Was she someone he'd been stalking? If it was random, he might have killed her to flush me out."

"Which is why we're gonna wait a tick to go back."

"But what if he escalates and kills someone else?"

"He can't when he's behind bars."

"He could hire someone," she said. "Or his grandmother could."

"I can't worry about anyone but you right now."

"Lincoln, I know you." She settled her hands on her hips. "If someone else gets hurt and you had the power to stop it, but didn't, it'll eat you up."

I pressed my palms to my eyes, trying to ward off a headache. "Jesus Christ."

"We need to head back to Harmony's."

"I really wanted you off your feet."

"And I will be. I'll work from the sofa."

I raised an eyebrow. "What about prenatal vitamins? Did you get those sorted?"

"Not yet."

"Lyric."

She sighed. "I promise, I'll look for an OB as soon as we get home."

"Get dressed," I ordered, pulling my phone out of my pocket and calling Doc.

"Hey."

"Hey. Lyric's pregnant," I said.

"No shit? Is that good news?"

"Yeah, brother, it's great news. We're stuck here for the moment, though, and I want her on prenatals and shit. Also, what can she take for morning sickness?"

"I can prescribe her prenatals until you guys get back. Send me the pharmacy information, and I'll send you a list of safe over the counter anti-nausea medications she can take."

"Thanks, brother."

"No problem," he said. "Happy for you, Doom."

I smiled. "Thanks, Doc."

I hung up and Lyric wrapped her arms around me. "My hero."

I chuckled. "Don't think I didn't see you steal a pair of my underwear."

"Like I said, my hero."

Kissing her gently, we cleaned up our breakfast dishes, then headed to her sister's.

Lyric

"Lyric," Doom growled.

"I'm going," I said, sitting back in the oversized chair in Harmony's office.

He'd just gotten back from the Fred Meyer pharmacy and handed me a prenatal vitamin and a bottled water. I'd taken advantage of his absence to stand behind Harmony and scan what evidence against Garrett she could find in the FBI database. But he'd caught me.

I took the pill and he leaned down to kiss me, sliding his tongue inside my mouth. "Just checking."

I couldn't stop a shiver. It reminded me of his threat at the benefit dinner and how much I wanted him to kiss me then.

He smiled. "I know what you're thinking."

"Yeah, I bet you do."

"You hungry?"

I wrinkled my nose and shook my head.

"You sick?"

"Just a little nausea. It'll pass."

"I'll be right back," he said.

"I cannot find anything else, LiLi," Harmony said. "He did it in the parking lot of the dealership."

"In front of the camera."

"Yes," Harmony confirmed.

"Damn it." I sighed. "The only reason he got caught with me was because my detail made some critical mistakes. I think he's trying to draw me out."

Harmony frowned. "Which is why you're staying here where he can't find you. Safe and sound."

I shook my head. "He's planning something."

"Probably."

"From jail?" Doom asked, handing me saltines and a soda.

"Thanks, honey," I said, taking them. "Yes. He has money, therefore, he has reach. And if he doesn't, Granny does. We need to go home."

"No," Doom and Harmony said in stereo.

"This needs to be done, once and for all."

Doom crossed his beefy arms and shook his head. "There's no way in hell I'm putting you and our child in the path of some psycho, Lyric."

"You'll keep me safe."

"I can't guarantee that unless we're at the compound. If you insist on going back to your house, there are too many variables. I can't lock it down."

I bit my lip. He had a point.

"*Or*, you can stay here where you're safe," Harmony stressed.

"He'll keep killing unless I come back. He did it before and I don't want anyone else to get hurt."

"He's locked up. He can't touch anyone right now."

"You of all people know there are prisoners who can do whatever the fuck they want from inside a cell," I countered. "He might not be able to do it personally, but he can pay someone else to do it. And what if they let him out on bail?"

"After killing a woman?" Doom snapped.

"If he pulls a judge his granny can buy, then it's possible."

"Jesus Christ," he hissed.

Harmony sighed. "I'm gonna have people on you, then."

"Dalton'll be able to put a team together," Doom said. "He's home for a while."

"Who's Dalton?" I asked.

"Dalton Moore. He used to work for the FBI, now he consults," Harmony said. "He splits his time between Savannah and Scotland. He and Jaxon work together on occasion."

"He's a friend to the club. I trust him," Doom said.

I nodded and met his eyes. "So, we can go home?"

He took a deep breath. "Yeah, Angel, we can go home."

"Give me two more days," Harmony begged.

I chuckled. "Okay, sissy, I can do that. My man's dragging his stuff here, though."

"Of course he is. The kids need to get to know their new uncle."

Doom kissed me quickly, then went to find a beer.

* * *

Doom left me at Harmony's and transferred his bag from the compound to the house just in time for dinner. He'd stopped on the way back to pick up beer, wine, and treats for the kids, so he'd further cemented himself into the hearts of my family, and I couldn't have loved him more for it. Well, I probably could have if he figured out a way to make wine safe to drink while pregnant, but since he wasn't a god, I'd have to settle for him being perfect in every other way.

Laying in bed later that night, I snuggled close and ran my finger across one of the flames of his tattoo and kissed his chest. "How did you get involved with your club?"

"Dustin, my lieutenant, actually lit that fire. Pun intended," he said. "Right after... ah... the accident, he decided to head back to Colorado. He's from there and left for various reasons I won't go into. He's in a club out there, Primal Howlers, and was called back in."

"Ooh, what's his super cool club name?"

Doom chuckled. "Moses."

"What do all of the patches on your vest mean?"

"Cut, baby."

"What?"

"It's called a cut. Not a vest. A vest is what Mr. Rogers wore."

"Mr. Rogers wore a cardigan."

He groaned. "Well, I don't wear either, so please never call my cut a vest."

I grinned. "Okay. Forget I asked. Go back to why you got into the club."

"The Howlers and the Dogs have been friendly for a while and Moses had asked Doc to check in on me after all the shit that went down. He knew I'd isolate, especially after I quit, and since Doc's like a fuckin' dog with a bone, pun also intended, he dragged me into the club. Rabbit came with me and the rest is history, as they say. We did a big reorg a few months ago, so my patch is now that of VP, instead of Road Captain, but otherwise, nothing's really changed."

"That's a promotion, right?"

"Yeah," he said.

"Congratulations."

"Thanks."

"So, who's who now?"

"Dash is Secretary and Badger's Treasurer. Doc's still prez and Alamo's still Sergeant, so that's really all that's changed. We're patchin' in a couple of the recruits next month."

"Who?"

"Mouse and Rabbit."

"Can I patch in?" I asked, throwing the covers back and straddling his hips.

"No chicks in the band, Angel. Sorry." He gripped my waist, lifting me slightly and guiding me onto his already hard cock.

I leaned over him and ran my tongue along his pulse. "Maybe this'll change your mind."

"Hard and fast rule, baby." He thrust up when he said, "Hard."

Kissing him again, I bit his lip. "How hard?"

He flipped me onto my back and dragged my hands above my head, pinning them to the mattress with one of his. "Hard."

He buried himself deep, kissing me even deeper, then rocked gently until I wrapped my legs around his waist and arched against him.

"Show me hard, baby," I begged, but instead of obliging, he pulled out of me and I growled in frustration.

"Shh, Angel, I'm gonna take care of you."

He kissed his way down my body, then he ran his tongue over my clit and through my soaked folds. Slipping two fingers inside of me, he swept my walls and I whimpered with need.

"You want it hard, baby?"

"Yes," I rasped.

"I want you on your knees, but I'm gonna keep my fingers right where they are. You think you can manage that?"

I nodded and we moved in tandem as I repositioned myself onto all-fours. He kissed my right butt cheek, his fingers moving inside of me again. "Good girl."

Slipping his digits out of me, he ran one against my tight hole and I licked my lips as I moaned. "When we get home and you're settled, I'm gonna play here. It'll be something for us to look forward to."

"Okay," I whispered, my body shivering with the promise. He guided his dick into me, squeezing my bottom. "Ready, Angel?"

"Yes," I hissed.

"Brace."

I braced and he slammed into me, harder and harder, over and over until I shoved my face in a pillow and screamed his name as I came. It took him a few more thrusts, and then we fell onto the mattress and he rolled us onto our sides in spoon fashion, kissing the nape of my neck gently. "I fucking love you, Lyric."

I grinned. "I fucking love you too, Lincoln."

His hand slid to my belly. "How's our baby?"

"So far so good." I closed my eyes, covering his hand with mine and linking our fingers. "Do you think he'll be okay?"

"*She'll* be perfect, Angel. I have no doubt we'll have a healthy and happy little blip who'll keep us up all night." He slid out of me and kissed my shoulder. "I'll be right back."

* * *

Doom

I cleaned up in the bathroom and walked back into the bedroom to find Lyric crying softly. "Angel, what's wrong?"

"I don't know," she said on a groan. "I'm just sad."

I forced back a chuckle and slid under the covers again, pressing a warm washcloth between her legs. "Come here."

She wrapped her arms around my neck and burrowed against me, kissing my throat. "I hate these fucking hormones, Doom. Seriously. I've cried more in the past few weeks than I have my entire life."

I lifted her chin and kissed her wet cheek. "Maybe this is Mother Nature's way of telling you it's time to let it all out."

"Are you ready for your woman to be a sobby, stabby mess

for the next six years?"

"Six years?"

"You said you want multiple kids, so…"

I chuckled. "Yeah, baby, if you're willin' to give me multiple kids, I'll take you sobby and stabby."

She smacked my chest. "Wrong answer."

"What's the right answer?"

"That you'll take me sobby and stabby, even if I wasn't willing to give you multiple kids."

I raised an eyebrow. "But that would be a lie."

Her mouth popped open in a gasp and I laughed.

"I'm kidding," I assured her. "Except for stabby. Sobby I can handle, stabby not so much."

"You're so lucky your dick's big."

I laughed. "Yeah?"

"Yeah." She smiled, finally, then yawned as she snuggled closer again.

"Sleep, baby. You've got a big day with Skyler tomorrow."

"'K."

"I love you, beautiful."

"I love you, too."

I held her until I heard her even breathing, then I let myself sleep as well.

* * *

Lyric

"I think this is it," I said, and Doom guided the rental into Hatch and Maisie's driveway. I'd spent the day with Harmony and Skyler getting mani-pedis and heaping attention on my niece who further wrapped her way around my heart. It was going to be even harder to leave in two days, but I was yearning for home, as was Doom.

Tonight, however, Doom had promised Maisie he'd join them for dinner and the invitation had been extended to me, which of course, I had no intention of turning down.

Lord, the chance to spend a few hours with two of the best looking men on the planet? Huh-uh, nope, not letting that oppor-

118

tunity pass me by.

"Well, this was not at all what I was expecting," I admitted as Doom parked the car.

Hatch's home was firmly ensconced in the suburbs, complete with neat lawn and a neighborhood that probably adhered to strict CC&Rs.

Doom chuckled and climbed out of the car, walking to my side and helping me out. He kissed me gently before grabbing the wine we'd bought, and then we made our way to the front door.

The door opened before we could knock and a flurry of blonde threw herself into Doom's arms. "Oh my god, I can't believe you're here."

Doom chuckled, handing the wine to me and hugging her back. "Hey, Poppy."

She pulled back and smiled up at him. "You look happy. Are you happy?"

"I'm happy, sweetheart."

She moved from him to me, pulling me in for a hug. "Thank you for making him happy."

I grinned. "You're welcome."

Hatch walked our way, grinning. "Maisie's in the kitchen," Hatch explained. "Come on back."

We followed him back and greeted their two boys, Jamie and Flash, who were on their way out. I'd met them last Christmas, and they didn't fall far from the tree of their father and I knew beyond a shadow of a doubt they were going to break hearts, if they weren't already.

Maisie handed Hatch a plate of the biggest steaks I'd ever seen, then hugged us both before guiding us to the large kitchen island. "Sit down and relax."

"Can I help?" I asked.

"No."

"Are you sure?" I pressed.

"Don't try," Poppy warned. "You'll get nowhere. Can I get you some wine?"

"Ah, no, thank you," I said. "Water's great."

Maisie gave me a secret smile, and I appreciated she hadn't

spilled the beans, so to speak.

"I'm gonna help Hatch with the meat," Doom said, and I raised an eyebrow.

"Do you think Hatch needs help with his meat?"

"He has a lot of meat, love," Maisie said. "He often needs help."

"Oh, really?"

"So much meat," Maisie said. "It's thick and he may need assistance getting it—"

"Mum!" Poppy snapped. "Enough talk about Dad's meat. I mean, *really*!"

Doom laughed out loud and headed out the back slider.

* * *

Doom

"Heard you needed some help with your meat," I said, closing the door behind me.

Hatch smirked, setting the empty platter on the table beside the grill. "My woman's tellin' stories again, huh?"

"Somethin' like that."

Hatch handed me a beer and I twisted the top and we clinked bottles.

"Congrats on VP," he said.

"Thanks, brother."

"You prepped on the Spider shit?"

"As much as I can be," I admitted. "Anything new?"

"No," Hatch said. "They're layin' low, which doesn't sit well with me. I've got feelers out, but you need to stay alert. They're plannin' something big, and I don't think Savannah's immune."

"Got it," I said. "Let 'em come. Fuckers need a lesson in manners."

Hatch raised an eyebrow. "Don't get cocky, Doom. That's when you're most vulnerable."

I sighed with a nod. He was probably right.

"How do you like yours?" he asked, pointing the tongs toward the steaks.

"Medium rare for me, medium for Lyric."

We put club business aside for lighter subjects and spent the rest of the evening getting to know the Wallace family. By the time I took Lyric home, we both felt we'd made life-long friends and neither of us could wait to come back to Portland.

FOURTEEN

Lyric

WE'D BEEN HOME for three days and I was settling in pretty easily. Garrett had, in fact, been granted bail, so Doom was on higher alert than before. Luckily, his trial was set for three weeks from now, so this whole issue would be resolved relatively quickly.

I'd moved a few things from my house into the compound yesterday, hard to do when your home was over six-thousand square feet and your man's space was less than a thousand.

Doc had insisted on clearing out one of the storage rooms so I could use it as an office and I'd initially thought it was a sweet gesture. Until I'd arrived downstairs that morning.

"There you are," I said to Doom, wrapping my arms around him and giving him a squeeze. He was currently making coffee, shirtless and in a pair of nicely fitting joggers. I had a feeling he was doing something physical because he wore a beanie, which he often did even when it was warm to keep his hair out of his face, and was a little sweaty. Delish. "I don't like waking up to an empty bed."

"Needed to finish something."

I met his eyes. "Everything okay?"

He smiled. "Yeah. I grabbed a couple more things from your place. I put them in your office."

"What was missing?"

He gave my butt a gentle smack. "Why don't you go look?"

I headed down the hall and pushed open the door, my hands going to my mouth to stop the girly squeal as I took in everything I was seeing.

Doom had basically replicated my home office. Although, because the space was twice that of the one at my house, he'd added a little lounge area with a television, my oversized snuggle chair and sofa, and a giant-ass cat tree for Booger... who was currently sitting in the cubby portion, staring at us like he was plotting our demise.

"Lincoln," I whispered, tears burning in the back of my throat as I turned and buried my face in his chest.

"I did good, huh?"

"Oh my god, you did so good. I can't believe you did all this."

"Doc and Alamo helped."

Doc's gesture so far surpassed 'kind.'

I wrapped my arms around Doom. "I can't believe Doc and Alamo and the rest of the guys worked like fiends to clear all this out just to make me feel comfortable."

"You're ours now, Angel." He smiled, stroking my cheek. "We protect what's ours, which means, we make them feel safe. This'll be your home away from home and we all want you to feel just as comfortable here as you do at your place."

I leaned up and kissed him. "I love you so hard."

He lifted me so I could wrap my legs around his waist, kicking the door shut and carrying me to my snuggle chair. He sat down and I shifted so I stayed straddling him, letting him slip my T-shirt over my head.

Kissing me again, he removed my bra and cupped my breasts, rolling my nipples into tight peaks, and I tugged his beanie off, freeing his hair and sliding my hands into it.

"Up, Angel," he directed, and I climbed off him, so he could stand.

We made quick work of removing the rest of our clothes and then he guided me back onto the chair, and onto his dick.

"Jesus," he hissed. "So fuckin' beautiful."

I smiled, leaning down to kiss him. "Thank you, Lincoln. For everything." I lifted, then lowered myself again. "Thank you for making me feel loved." I lifted. "Thank you for making me feel safe." Then lowered. "Thank you for working your ass off to make my life easier." Up again, then down. "But most of all, thank you for being you. You are as close to perfect as a human can get, honey, and I won't ever take you for granted."

I gripped the back of the chair and rocked gently, taking him deep and relishing the feeling of him inside of me, then I rode him. Hard.

Doom thrust up as I moved, driving himself even deeper and the sound of skin against skin drove me even more crazy as a climax began to build. He slid a hand between us and fingered my clit and I lost all control, my walls contracting around his cock as he cupped my breasts and buried his face between them.

"I need you to do somethin' for me," he said.

I stroked his beard. "Anything."

"You need to figure out a wedding."

"What do you mean?"

"We're gettin' married before this baby comes. I'm fine with a quickie on the courthouse steps, but if you want a weddin', you need to plan it ASAP."

I climbed off him and snagged my panties off the floor, shimmying them on. "First, you haven't asked. Second, getting married isn't going to change anything."

"Are you saying you're not going to marry me?"

"Refer to first point," I said.

He raised an eyebrow. "Don't verbally spar with me, Lyric."

I sighed. "I have never entertained the thought of marriage."

"Entertain it."

"Doom—"

"Lyric, you're havin' my child."

"Stop interrupting me!" I snapped.

He pushed his hair back and secured it with a band, then the beanie again. "I will propose to you if that's what you want, but if you want a big wedding you need to start planning now."

I felt tears of frustration form. God, these pregnancy hormones were starting to piss me off. I was typically as even-keeled as they came and I rarely cried.

"Why do we have to get married?"

"Jesus! Because you're having my kid!" he growled.

"People who are unmarried have kids all the time," I countered.

"Ly—" Before he could release the rage I was sure he was fixin' to, his phone buzzed and he let out a curse as he answered it. "Hey, Pop, now's kind of a bad time. What? When? Shit. Yeah, I'll be right there." He slid his phone into his pocket. "My dad's had an accident."

"Oh my god, is he okay?"

"I think so. He needs me to run by his place."

I nodded. "Okay."

Doom sighed, sliding his hand to my neck and pulling me against him. "I love you, Angel, and I don't know what's got you spooked, but we're gonna figure it out, because this baby's comin' into this world with his mother and father hitched."

I bit my lip, but didn't respond.

He kissed me quickly. "I'll see you in a bit."

* * *

Doom

I pulled up to my dad's place, which was also my childhood home, and headed inside. "Pop?"

"Kitchen!" he called.

He was sitting at the table, a dish towel wrapped around his hand, a pair of wire cutters and pliers sitting next to him, and his face was as pale as a sheet. "What the fuck did you do?" He unwrapped the towel and I hissed out, "Shit."

"I can't get the ring off."

"Why the hell didn't you go to emergency?" I admonished.

"Not wastin' my money. I just need you to cut it off for me. But be careful. I gotta try and save it."

"Jesus, Dad, you're insane." I washed my hands and studied the wound. "What happened?"

"I was changing a fuse and missed the live wire next to it. The damn thing sent an arc and fused the ring to my finger."

"I coulda had Doc bring his shit," I said as I slid the wire cutters under the band as gently as I could.

"Don't wanna waste his time." He grimaced as I snipped the gold and set the cutters down. "Sorry I pulled you away."

"It's okay, Pop. This was more important." I used the pliers to pull the ring away from the skin and once it was free, I loaded his hand up with triple antibiotic ointment, then bandaged it.

"Thanks," Dad said.

"Did you get the fuse changed?" I asked, throwing the bandage remnants away.

"No."

"Basement?"

"Yeah."

"Okay, I'll take care of it," I said. "Take some ibuprofen or Tylenol while I do that."

"Thanks, Bud."

I headed down to the basement and saw the exposed wire he was talking about, so I capped it, then changed the fuse that was blown before checking the others. After clearing away the mess and putting away the tools my dad had left laying around, I headed back upstairs to find him with a beer in one hand and an open one waiting for me.

He waved to the seat across from him. "Did you work it out with your woman?"

"Yeah." I flopped into the seat and took a long pull from the bottle. "She's home. At the compound for the moment." I studied the table. "She's pregnant."

"Wow," he said quietly. "You okay?"

"She's refusin' to marry me."

126

"No kiddin'?"

"Yeah." I sighed. "You interrupted that argument when you called."

He chuckled. "My timing's always been perfect."

I smiled. "Maybe so."

"Where are you at with Jennifer and Ezra?"

I waited for pain to slice through my chest, but what came was just bittersweet memories instead. "It's better, Pop. Lyric's changed everything."

He smiled, reaching over to squeeze my arm. "I'm real proud of you, son."

"Thanks, Dad," I rasped, and took another sip of my beer. "Why don't you come by the club tonight and eat with us? Doc can look at your hand and you can meet Lyric."

"I can do that."

I stood and dumped the rest of my beer, then threw the bottle in the recycling bin. Dad followed me out to my bike and hugged me.

"Six," I said, and he nodded, before I climbed on and took off.

Arriving back at the compound, I walked in and found Willow and Jasmine in the kitchen cooking, and opened the fridge for a beer. "Either of you seen Lyric?"

"I think she's in her office," Willow said.

"Thanks."

"Hey," she called, as I started to leave. I faced her and she smiled. "I'm really glad you pulled your head out of your butt."

I dropped my head back and laughed. "Me too, sweetheart." I rushed her, pulling her in for a bear hug.

"Doom! I've got flour all over my hands."

"Don't give a fuck."

She wiped her hands on my back and giggled. "You asked for it."

I kissed her cheek and headed off to find my woman, flour covered and all. I pushed open the office door and found her curled up in her snuggle chair, sound asleep. Her laptop was still on her lap, but it was closed, so I lifted it from her and set it on the coffee table.

She started slightly, reaching for it.

"It's just me, baby. I got it," I said.

"Is your dad okay?"

"Yeah. I'll spare you the gory details, but he's good." I knelt in front of her. "Tell me why you're freaked about marrying me."

"It's not you."

"Yeah, I get that."

She let out a frustrated groan and dragged her hands down her face.

"Angel, just spit it out. Don't filter it."

"You're going to need to sign a prenup."

"Okay."

"Wait," she said. "Really?"

"Yeah," I said. "But just so you know. I'm not going to ask you to sign one in return."

She glanced around the room and it hit me.

And that was when I realized she really hadn't read the file her man had gotten on me.

"Jesus," I said, and laughed.

"What?"

I walked to her desk and retrieved the manila envelope from under some of her random papers handing it to her. "I give you permission to read everything in this. In fact, I'd rather you did before you spend one more second freaking out over shit you don't need to freak out over."

I leaned down and kissed her gently.

"I'm gonna go take a shower while you do that."

* * *

Lyric

Twenty minutes later…

The sneaky, son of a bitch!

I dropped the paperwork on the coffee table and stalked upstairs to our room, letting myself in and finding Doom walking out of the bathroom. "You're fucking loaded?" I snapped.

He chuckled. "Yep."

"You have more money than I do."

"I have more *cash* than you do. Your assets exceed mine by almost a million with your house, but yeah, we're pretty equal in that regard."

"Why do you live... *here?*" I demanded, then realized I sounded like I was insulting his home, which wasn't nice. "I mean, not that it's not a nice place and I'm so grateful for the safe space to be."

He grinned. "Baby, it's okay. I get it. Women want a home to settle in. I had that, but when it was ripped away from me, I couldn't go back, so I packed it up and sold it. I kept a few things I couldn't part with at Dad's, but sold everything else and threw everything into stocks and bonds. Rabbit's a fuckin' genius with that kind of shit, so my money's tripled a few times over. Not to mention, Jen's life insurance that paid double because it was an accident. My business does well and since my dues cover my room here, and I really didn't need more than a bed and place to eat, everything I needed was here, so here I stayed. I have no overhead, so I have next to no expenses. My bike's paid for, and if I need to drive something else, I've got a couple loaners at the shop."

"I'm sorry, honey. I didn't want to sound like it was about money, because I really don't care what you make. I love all of you, no matter what. It's just all the crap I went through trying to keep Melody's exes from taking her for everything she has was a nightmare, and I swore prenups would be airtight and signed before any of us got married. Jaxon signed his without any issue, so I don't know why I would have thought you'd be a dick about it."

"Probably because you thought I didn't own a home and didn't have a pot to piss in, so there was a possibility, no matter how much we loved each other, that it could go bad, and then everything you'd worked so hard for would be ripped away." He stroked my cheek. "Much like when you were just starting out as a young woman and the chance of having a family of your own was ripped away in an instant."

I blinked back tears. "How do you know how to put all of my feelings into words?"

He chuckled. "I'm the Lyric whisperer."

"God, I love you."

"Love you too."

"You gonna marry me?"

"You haven't asked me."

He grinned, leaning down to kiss me. "If I ask you properly, are you going to say yes?"

"You better make it fast because I want a proper wedding before I start showing." I tugged on the towel, releasing the knot. "For now, though, you're going to do more of what you did this morning."

FIFTEEN

Lyric

"**O**H MY GOD, Lincoln, why the hell didn't you start with, 'my dad's coming for dinner'?" I admonished as we were laying in bed after he'd given me three mind-blowing orgasms.

"Because then this wouldn't have happened."

"Well, you're right about that," I grumbled, scrambling off the bed. "What am I going to wear?"

"Wear the silver dress you wore to girls' night."

I rolled my eyes. "That's a little dressy."

"Easy access to your pussy, though."

"Oh my god, if you try to get at my pussy while your dad is here, I'm going to smack you." I stepped into his closet. "I think I may have an old chastity belt in here somewhere."

Doom laughed and leaned against the doorframe as I rum-

131

maged through my clothes.

"Wear what's comfortable."

"I need to go shopping."

"We can do that this week."

I bit my lip as I continued to throw fabric around the closet. "I should probably look for a car as well."

"Do you know what you want?"

"Probably a Volvo," I said distractedly.

"I'm good with that. I'll start looking for one."

I faced him. "I want a new one, though. Bells and whistles, Doom. I like bells and whistles."

"You just totaled a 1992 VW Passat, and you're telling me you like bells and whistles?"

"It's the only thing in my life that didn't have bells and whistles," I pointed out. "It was my grandma's and she gave it to me before she died."

"Ah," he said. "Now I get it."

I nodded.

"That's why you held onto it for so long."

"Yes."

He smiled. "Okay, baby, we'll get you a Volvo with bells and whistles. But I'm still gonna get you a deal."

"I can live with that."

"Wear the blue," he said, pointing to the shirt in my right hand. "It matches your eyes."

I nodded. "Okay."

He stepped inside and kissed me gently. "He's gonna love you. Trust me."

I nodded. "I've never met parents before."

"Never?"

I shook my head. "It's never gotten this far before."

"You love me, right?"

I smiled. "So much."

"He raised me. Mom died when I was sixteen."

"Oh, god, honey, I'm so sorry."

"It wasn't fun. He still wears his ring. Well, he did. I had to cut it off his finger today because the dumbass didn't cap a live wire off before touching it."

I grimaced. "Ouch."

"Exactly. He still loves my mom, but he didn't do what I did. He didn't go into a dark hole and fester. I wish I'd taken a page out of his book a little sooner."

I slid my hands up his chest. "If Ezra had lived, honey, you would have. I'm sure of it. If your dad had lost you *and* your mom, he might not have fared as well as you did. I mean, I couldn't imagine losing you now, but I bet you were an amazing child."

He chuckled. "I was hell on wheels."

"Oh, I have no doubt about that." I smiled. "But beautiful, nonetheless. I wonder how many girls had pregnancy scares after a night with you."

"None. No glove, no love, baby."

"Well, you were pretty quick to unpeel for me."

He leaned closer. "And you and Jennifer are the only two women I've ever done that with."

I couldn't stop a quiet gasp. "Really?"

"Yeah." Doom slid his hand to my neck and stroked my pulse. "Whether it was subconscious or not, I was just waiting for you to calm the rage in me."

"You think so?"

He nodded. "I knew it the night I told you about Jen and Ezra. You pulled me back from the brink and I could actually breathe after speaking their names. That hadn't happened before. It's why I freaked."

"Honey," I whispered, searching his eyes. "I see you. I have always seen you."

He smiled. "I know. That also freaked me the hell out."

"God, I love you."

"Back atya. I'm gonna go let Doc know Dad will need him to look at his hand real quick."

"Okay. I'll just be here freaking out about meeting your dad."

He patted my butt with a laugh. "He's gonna love you. Promise."

Then he walked out of the room.

133

Doom never came back to the room, so I made my way downstairs once I was dressed and went looking for him. He was in the great room, talking to a man who had his back to me and I assumed this was his dad, but when he turned I just about had a heart attack. "Oh my god, *Sterling?*"

"Hey, sweetheart," he said, opening his arms for me. "How are you enjoying the sunroom?"

I walked in for a hug. "Honestly, Booger uses it a lot more than I do."

"You two know each other?" Doom asked.

"He pretty much rebuilt my house," I said.

"Jesus," Doom hissed. "You knew it was her all along, didn't you, old man?"

Sterling shrugged. "Not a whole lotta Lyric's in Savannah, bud, so, yeah, I figured."

"You didn't think to clue me in?"

"And miss seeing the look on your face right now? Not a chance in hell."

I bit back a smile as Doom turned to me. "And you. How did you not put two-and-two together that we were related? Just how many Marxx's are there in Savannah."

"I had no idea his last name was Marxx," I said. "His company's Sterling Restoration. He introduced himself as Sterling and I just figured he went by his last name or he was one of those cool guys that only has one name. You know, like Bono... or Cher."

Even though he was obviously a little irked, he laughed. "Are your cool guy references really limited to Bono and Cher?"

I rolled my eyes. "Well, no, because obviously, I know Sterling."

"Damn straight," Sterling retorted. "Besides, Cher and that Bono fella aren't together anymore. Didn't he hit a tree or something?"

I glanced at Doom and we both burst out laughing.

"That was Sonny, Pop," Doom explained. "And he wasn't with Cher when that happened."

I wrinkled my nose. "Rest in peace, Sonny."

"You gonna let go of my woman, Pop?" Doom complained.

Sterling gave me a gentle squeeze. "In a minute."

Doom was having none of that, taking my hand and pulling me gently away from his father. I chuckled. "There's plenty of me to go around."

"Like hell there is."

"Hey, Pop," Doc said, walking into the room. "Heard you were a dumbass."

Sterling chuckled. "Guilty."

"Come on back to my office and I'll take a look."

As they left, I wrapped my arms around Doom.

"You look gorgeous," he said.

I wore a pair of faded skinny jeans and the dark blue, off the shoulder chamber top he'd suggested, along with a pair of blingy flipflops.

"Thanks, honey." I smiled up at him. "But if I'd known your dad was Sterling, I wouldn't have freaked out as much."

He chuckled. "Baby, you freak too much about a lot of things you don't need to freak out about. I'm learning it's your process."

"Oh, really?"

"Keeps you humble."

"Dork." I stood on tiptoes and kissed him. "I'm going to help the girls with dinner."

"Okay."

I walked into the kitchen and Willow was cheesing up some kind of casserole, while Jasmine was tossing a salad and Olivia was opening a bottle of wine.

"Can I help?" I asked.

"Can you grab plates, please?" Willow asked

"Of course," I said, stepping into the pantry.

"Kids are eating," Quin said, walking in just as I set plates on the island. "The guys have them, and I told them it's going to take us at least ten more minutes to finish what we're doing."

"No, it's not," Willow countered.

"*Yes*, it is," Quin said, flapping her hand toward the bottle of wine Olivia had just opened.

"Oh," Willow said with a giggle. "Right. Yes it is. In fact, I should probably add more cheese and melt it on this mac and cheese."

While Willow added more cheddar, Quin poured everyone else a glass of wine, and me a glass of sprite, then we toasted to the men who took care of our babies so we could hide in the kitchen and drink.

Once the mac and cheese was done, we started to carry things to the smaller table in the great room. It was just a few of us tonight and I liked that just fine, especially, because I got a chance to watch the dynamic between Doom and his dad, and it was amazing.

Their banter was easy, and they were obviously good friends, but Doom's respect for the man who raised him was evident, and his southern raisin' had been done right. I couldn't wait to watch Doom with our babies, and I was so grateful they'd have a grandparent in their life.

Doom slid an arm around my waist and kissed my temple. "You good?"

I smiled. "So good."

He went back to his conversation with Alamo and I focused on Kinsey who was telling me all about her day playing with Booger.

SIXTEEN

Lyric

TWO DAYS LATER, I gripped Doom's hand as we walked into the restaurant after a day of shopping. He'd organized a dinner with Dalton Moore and his wife, because it was time to lock down a detail so that I didn't feel as though I was imprisoned at the club.

I'd never met any of Doom's friends outside of the club, and Dalton was both a friend of Jaxon's and Doom's. Dalton was actually a friend of several of the Dogs'. He seemed to have become an honorary member, although, Doom said if anyone said that, he might shoot them to keep it off the FBI's radar.

The hostess led us to our table and Doom introduced me to Dalton and his wife, Andi. Dalton was tall, muscular and looked a bit like the Polo model in magazines. Andi was blonde and curvy and sassy as all get out. I loved her instantly.

"My sister and brother-in-law are in town," Dalton said. "So I hope it's okay if they join us for dessert. She's dying for some downhome company."

I grinned. "Fine by me. Where do they live?"

"Scotland."

"Oh, wow. I love Scotland," I said. "I've been a couple of times to visit Melody when she's been performing. But, there's really nowhere like Savannah, so I can understand wanting that downhome company."

We took our seats and Doom slid his arm over the back of my chair, stroking my hair as we studied our menus.

Before the server came to take our drink orders, however, a rather frazzled woman came rushing in, her eyes focused on Andi. "Sorry, I'm late!"

"Fuck," Doom breathed out.

The woman must have heard him because she looked his way and stopped so hard, she nearly fell flat on her face. "Doom?"

Doom stood and gave her an apologetic smile. "Hey, Aspen."

She glanced at me, then him, then back to me. I rose to my feet and thrust out my hand. "I'm Lyric."

She shook my hand, but kept her eyes on Doom. Then she pulled her hand from mine, stepped up to Doom, and punched him in the face.

"Oh my god!" Andi squealed. "Aspen!"

"Hey!" I growled.

She made a move to do it again, but Doom caught her wrists and dragged them behind her back. "Nope. Let's go talk. Excuse us, everyone. We'll be right back." He physically walked her out of the restaurant, and I was left at the table, in shock, alone with his friends.

* * *

Doom

I led Aspen outside and down toward the water. She was crying now, but I could tell she was trying not to completely lose her shit.

"I have a lot to make up for," I started.

"You're an asshole."

"I am."

"Six years, Doom. *Six*." She faced me, crossing her arms. "We were friends. Close friends. You fucking threw that away because I told you the truth."

I dragged my hands down my face. "I know, sweetheart. There's no excuse."

"I know there's no fucking excuse, Doom! That doesn't make it right." She slapped at her cheeks, the tears flowing freely now. "I miss you."

"You could have called me."

"You were in the wrong!"

I sighed. "I know. The whole thing was all kinds of fucked up."

"I thought you were dead."

"No you didn't."

She rolled her eyes. "You don't know what I thought."

I crossed my arms. "Babe, if you really thought I was dead, you would have stormed every funeral home in order to get the last word in or do something nasty to my corpse."

Her mouth twitched and I could tell I'd hit a nerve.

She sighed, leaning against the railing protecting us from falling onto the rocks. "Who's Lyric?"

"She's the woman who saved me."

"Aw, honey, did she really?" she rasped.

I nodded. "Not sure how it happened, but she did."

Aspen's eyes filled with tears again and she rushed me. I caught her, pulling her close and hugging her as she wrapped her arms around me. "I'm so happy for you. Oh my god, you deserve to be happy. Finally."

"She's pregnant, Aspen."

She pulled back and met my eyes. "No shit?"

"No shit."

She grinned. "Congratulations."

"Thanks."

Pulling away, she wiped her tears. "God, she must think I'm

a total crazy bitch."

I smiled. "Obviously not enough to follow us out here and demand answers."

"Is she good to you?"

"Better than I deserve."

"You deserve a lot, Doom," she said.

"How about you?" I nodded to her left hand which had a rock the size of Houston on it.

She smiled. "I met the man of my dreams and married him before he could run. I'm actually on my way to meet him."

"You're not staying for dinner?"

"No. I needed to drop something off to Andi, and get my arms around her since she just flew in. It's our tradition." She smiled. "I refuse to let more than twelve hours go before seeing her when she flies in, even if it's just for a hug, then we set up a girls' day."

"I love that you make your friendships a priority, Aspen. I'm sorry I took that for granted."

"Oh, you didn't take it for granted, buddy. You broke it, then stomped the shit out of it."

"Guilty." I grimaced. "Will you forgive me?"

"Of course I'll forgive you, you idiot. But you owe me."

"I figured." I smiled. "If you feel like you don't need to hit me again, maybe we can go back in."

"I'm good," she said.

I rubbed my jaw. "You punch hard, woman."

She grinned. "I was pissed."

"Yeah, I got that." I hooked my arm around her neck and pulled her to me, guiding her back into the restaurant.

* * *

Lyric

Doom and Aspen returned, their arms around each other and I felt a pang of jealousy, but like a good southern woman, I buried it deep. Even Andi looked a little embarrassed for me, and there was nothing worse than having someone embarrassed *for* you.

"Lyric, I'm so sorry," Aspen said, taking her seat. "Doom

had that coming and I'm sure he'll explain why later, but let me just say, I'm so glad you two are happy. Congratulations on the baby."

I raised an eyebrow at Doom. We'd made the decision to keep the pregnancy on the downlow with the general public until we knew I was in the clear and the baby was healthy.

Andi widened her eyes at Aspen who looked confused, and I just wanted to crawl into a hole and die.

"Ah, thank you," I said.

I was about to excuse myself to go to the restroom when a tall, very regal looking man walked in with a gorgeous brunette...whom I recognized.

"Oh, my word," I breathed out. "Dr. Gunnach?"

"Lyric?"

I nodded and Samantha Gunnach pulled me in for a huge hug. "How are you?"

"Well, I'm incredible thanks to you."

"Oh?"

"I'm pregnant."

She clapped her hands, tears forming. "Oh, lovey, that's amazing." She hugged me again. "I'm so glad."

"Dr. Warner told me it was impossible."

"Did she?" She gave me a gentle smile. "I'm sorry I wasn't there for that meeting. I was called away that morning with another emergency and had to head back to Scotland."

"Yes, Dr. Warner mentioned that."

"I did ask her to warn you that it would be unlikely you'd be able to conceive, but I never like to take away the option for a miracle to happen, because sometimes hope is a powerful healing tool."

"Well, whatever you did surgically was all the hope I needed."

"I'm so glad, Lyric. Truly."

"Doom," I said. "This is the surgeon who made our baby possible."

Samantha reached out to shake his hand, but Doom pulled her in for a hug instead. "First and foremost, thank you for saving her life."

"This is actually my sister," Dalton said.

"Oh, wow," I breathed out. "I'm sorry, would y'all give me a minute. I just need some air."

"Of course," Samantha said, and I headed for the door.

I walked down to where I could watch the water and took several deep breaths, trying to sort out exactly what I was feeling.

"She's an old friend, and I treated her like shit," Doom said.

"An old girlfriend," I said to the water because I couldn't look at him.

"Not really. We fucked, but there was nothing there, which she reminded me when she ended it. She's good people, honey, and I ghosted her six years ago. Tonight, she told me her opinion on that."

I finally faced him with a sigh. "Do you have feelings for her?"

"No." He raised his hands in surrender. "Not now, not ever. We were really great friends and I fuckin' blew it with her. I treated her like shit, as I'm sure you can imagine. I have some atoning to do, but tonight was a good start."

I crossed my arms. "What kind of atoning?"

"She'll probably make me give her a year of free oil changes or some shit like that."

"So, nothing... personal."

He smiled, closing the distance between us and sliding his hand to my neck, stroking my pulse. "Depends on what you mean by personal. She's married, Angel. And really happy, as am I. If you don't want me to have anything to do with her, I'll cut all ties, but she's no threat to you, and she's a fuckin' phenomenal friend. She'll be the same to you."

"I would never ask you to cut ties with a friend, Doom. I trust you. I was just a little shocked when we'd made the decision about keeping the baby secret for the moment and she blurted it out to a table full of strangers."

"Yeah, I'm sorry about that." He lifted my chin. "I haven't been a good man, Angel. For a long time I've let people down. I want to make it right with the people who mean something to me."

I wrapped my arms around his waist. "Baby, I'm all in. I'll be by your side, at your back, under you, on your dick, whatever you need."

He chuckled, leaning down to kiss me. "Love you."

"Love you, too. Now feed us. Your baby's hungry."

SEVENTEEN

Lyric

THE FOLLOWING WEDNESDAY, I had my first OB appointment, so Doom left work early and picked me up. We headed to the clinic and the doctor poked and prodded, checking my previous ultrasound the hospital in Portland had faxed over, declaring I was about nine weeks along. I already knew that, so we prepared for our little miracle to arrive in about seven months.

I couldn't wait for all this crap with Garrett to be dealt with so I could go home. Doom had given me a concessional pass to check in once a week, just to make sure my house was still standing, and today was that day. He wanted to get in anyway and start measuring for the nursery.

I had no idea where to even start with what to buy for a

nursery, but luckily, I had my sister and the club women to help me. Everything was starting to become real for me and I was finally allowing myself to get excited.

Our 'detail' today consisted of Rabbit and Dash, along with two agents Dalton had set up, who immediately cleared the back and side yards. Once they were satisfied no one was lurking, Rabbit stood with me in the foyer while Doom, Dash, and the agents checked every nook and cranny of my house.

"All clear," Doom declared, jogging down my stairs, Dash following.

The agents walked out from different parts of the downstairs, agreeing, and then Doom and I were left alone.

The agents planned to walk the perimeter, while Dash and Rabbit hung out on the porch, so Doom and I could do what we needed and get out.

"I miss my house," I said with a sigh.

"As soon as this shit's sorted, you'll be back in it," Doom promised, leading me up the stairs. At the top, he faced me. "I'm gonna barrel over you if you don't stop me."

I grinned. "Yeah, I'm picking up on that."

"I'm thinkin' the baby's room should be next to the master."

"That room is currently full of everything I haven't had a chance to—" He pushed open the door and I gasped. "Oh my god." The room was empty. "Where is everything?"

"Sorted and stacked in the basement."

"When?"

"When we came to get your office packed up. Olivia inventoried everything, then directed a few of the recruits to pack it up. If you want shit moved somewhere else, let me know and we'll take care of it."

"I swear, I feel like I'm gonna owe those women a kidney at this rate."

He chuckled and pushed me gently further into the room. "Start thinking about colors and what you want in here."

He pulled out a measuring tape and his phone and started taking notes.

"I don't know the first thing about babies, Doom. I have no idea what we're going to need."

"That's what a registry's for," he said distractedly. "We'll hit a Target or that little boutique downtown and start throwing shit on it."

I nodded, but the enormity of this responsibility was sinking in and I started to panic a little.

"Hey," he said, gently, suddenly standing in front of me.

"Hmm?"

He lifted my chin and smiled. "You've got this. You're gonna be a phenomenal mom, Lyric. Don't start doubting yourself now."

I dropped my face to his chest and wrapped my arms around his waist. "I just feel like I turned that side off when I thought it would never happen, you know?"

"You're gonna rock this, you'll see."

"I hope so."

He kissed me gently, then slid something out of his pocket and knelt in front of me. "Okay, Angel, rubber meets road time. Will you marry me?"

He held up the sweetest sapphire and diamond ring I'd ever seen and I smiled. "Yes. This is beautiful, where did you get it?"

"It was my great grandmother's," he said, sliding it on my finger, and standing. "Dad brought it over when he came for dinner. He knows how much you love antiques and since this belonged to his mother's mother, he thought it should go to you."

My eyes filled with tears as I nodded. "Oh my god, you Marxx men are... I don't know... so incredibly irresistible."

"You think so?" He smiled. "If you want something else, I'll buy it for you, you just let me know."

"No. I love it. It's perfect. You're perfect." I stroked his beard. "I love you. And I love your dad. Thank you."

He leaned down and kissed me. "We should get goin'. You've got a wedding to plan."

I chuckled. "I have a case to prepare for."

"You have a case to prep for and a wedding to plan."

"Hold on," I ordered. "You *are* going to help me with this wedding, right?"

"You tell me what you need and I'll do it, Angel, but if you ask me about colors, my opinion will always be black."

I laughed. "Okay, got it."

"And I'm not wearin' a tux."

I wrinkled my nose. "But you'd look so *hot* in a tux."

"Non-negotiable."

"Kilt?"

"Not wearin' a skirt, Lyric."

"It's not a skirt, Doom, it's a kilt."

He raised an eyebrow. "No."

"Kimono?"

"Are you Japanese?" he challenged.

"I could be, somewhere in my history," I said. "I don't know. I haven't done that DNA swab thingy yet."

He shook his head. "No kimono."

"Could we discuss lederhosen?"

"Jesus," he hissed on a laugh. "No."

"But you'd look so cute in those little shorts."

Before he could comment, a deafening explosion sounded and I was suddenly thrown against the wall.

* * *

Doom

I turned to answer Lyric and was sent back to my heels by a shockwave that rippled through the room. My first instinct was that someone had driven into the house, but the ringing in my ears told me there had been an explosion.

I ran to Lyric and covered her body with mine.

"Are you okay?" I called out through the thick haze of smoke now filling the room.

"What was that?" she asked, and I struggled to hear her through the high-pitched squeal in my head.

"I have to get you out of here." I helped Lyric to her feet and shielded her as I guided us to the hallway and to the kitchen. That's when I saw the epicenter of the explosion. Something or someone had blown a hole through the roof of the garage and part of the kitchen.

"My beautiful house!" Lyric cried.

147

"Right now, my only concern is for you. Now, stay low. This could all be his way of drawing you out into the open," I said.

"*His* way?" Lyric asked. "Do you mean, Garrett?"

"Who else is trying to kill you?"

"But he's in jail," Lyric said.

"I know, Angel. We can talk about this later. Right now, I need to get you out of this house, so please stay low and don't make a move or a sound unless I say so."

I felt her nod her head under my arm.

"Doom!" I heard Dash call out.

"We're in here!" I replied. "What the fuck happened?"

"There was a drone. It dropped something on the house. Rabbit's hurt!"

"We're coming out. Make sure you have your eyes open and keep us covered," I replied and carefully led Lyric out the front door. Dash and Rabbit were on the front porch, which like them, had clearly seen better days.

The entire right side of Rabbit's body was covered in black soot, and most of his clothes on that side had disintegrated. He had what looked to me like serious burn marks on his neck, arm and upper thigh.

"I'm okay. Just a little crispy," Rabbit replied.

"He was standing pretty close to the house when that thing hit us," Dash said.

I scanned the area as we moved closer to the street but didn't see anyone except for Lyric's neighbors, who were now coming out of their houses to investigate the explosion. Whoever was operating the drone was long gone, if he was ever in the area to begin with. Who knows what this sick fuck had planned?

"We need to get him to a hospital, pronto," I said to Dash.

"I'm okay," Rabbit said. "Doc can patch me up."

"You're in shock, and we need to get you an ambulance before it wears off." I pulled my phone from my pocket, but a neighbor must have already called 9-1-1 as the sound of approaching sirens filled the air.

Debris was scattered across the front lawn and a section of the rain gutter had been torn from the house, launched through the air, and was now imbedded in the front windshield of Lyric's

148

new Volvo.

"My car," she cried.

I held Lyric tight. "It's okay, Angel. I can fix your car, and Dad'll get a crew on the house right away."

"I don't care about any of that right now. I just want our baby to be safe," Lyric said with a sadness that both broke my heart and filled me with rage.

I looked down and locked eyes with her. "I promise you'll never be unsafe again. I'm going to find whoever is helping Smalls and burn him to the ground. I'll get to the bottom of how he was able to get to you this time and make sure it's never able to happen again."

My phone buzzed just as the first emergency vehicles began to arrive. It was Doc and I almost didn't answer, given the situation, but he wasn't the kind of guy to call just to chit chat, so I decided it was probably best to answer.

"Kind of in the shit right now, Doc. What's up?"

"Hatch just called to give us a head's up. The Spiders are making moves against the Dogs all over the country. Not just us, but the Presidents, Howlers, and anyone else that's backing the Burning Saints. It looks like one of the Saints has already been taken out, so be careful...do I hear sirens?"

"I think Hatch was a little too late," I said.

"What the fuck happened?" Doc demanded.

I filled him in on what I knew, growing angrier by the second.

"Goddammit. The women are locked down, right fuckin' now!"

"Yeah, brother," I agreed. "You gonna handle that?"

"Yeah. I'll put the call out, then talk to Hatch and Minus."

Minus was the president for the Burning Saints' and coincidentally, Hatch's brother-in-law.

"We'll convene in an hour. All hands."

"Okay," I said, and hung up.

"Doom," Lyric rasped.

"Yeah, baby?"

"I'm gonna—"

She pulled away and promptly puked all over the ground.

"Local PD's gonna be here imminently," Dash warned. "You need to get Lyric back to the compound. Gator's takin' care of Willow, so I'll deal with Rabbit and Dalton's men'll deal with the cops."

I nodded, and guided Lyric out to the street where I texted Mouse to come get us.

* * *

Lyric

Doom buckled me into the back of the car Mouse drove, then slid in beside me. We drove back to the compound in silence and Doom led me up to our room where I promptly rushed to the bathroom and threw up everything I'd eaten in the last year. Well, everything I hadn't already puked up on my porch.

While I was losing my lunch, chaos was ensuing outside our bedroom. I could tell Doom was trying to keep it from me, but I could also tell he was as freaked as I was, he was just better at hiding it than me.

"Baby, Willow's gonna hang with you for a bit while the brothers meet," Doom said from the doorway.

"I'm okay, Doom. She doesn't need to do that."

"It's not really up for discussion," Willow called out, her sweet voice hiding the bossy lioness hidden inside.

Doom kissed the top of my head. "If you need me, I'm here, okay? But try not to need me for a bit. I'm going to send Doc up to check on you in a few."

"Okay, honey," I whispered, and he left me.

Once my stomach calmed, I brushed my teeth and walked into my bedroom. Willow sat in the chair by the window, studying her phone. She smiled up at me and nodded toward the dresser. "I grabbed Sprite and saltines."

"I love you," I said.

"Are you okay?"

"I think so. Doc's going to check me over in a few, but I don't think anything's hurt."

"Well, Doom wants you in bed," she said.

I rolled my eyes. "Of course he does."

"Now," she bossed.

I groaned. "I'm going."

I slid under the covers and settled the pillows behind my back so Willow and I could at least visit for a while.

EIGHTEEN

Doom

Two hours later…

"**F**IRST OF ALL, I want to let you all know Rabbit is gonna be okay," Doc said. "He's at Memorial and they happen to have one of the best burn units in the country."

Despite his words of assurance, Doc looked like he'd aged five years over night.

"He's got second, and third degree burns up and down his body and is going to require a series of grafts over the next six months. It's gonna be rough, but we all know Rabbit is a tough kid."

"The good news is, for once it wasn't Dash who got hurt, so

Willow doesn't have to tear the club a new asshole once again," I said to chuckles around the room.

"How are Lyric and the baby?" Alamo asked.

"Doing great. Resting safely upstairs," I replied.

"Glad to hear it," Alamo replied, and then the pleasantries were over.

Doc hit the gavel on the table and the room settled.

"Brothers, if you haven't noticed, we're now at war," Doc said. "Over the past twenty-four hours, the Spiders have made it clear they're out for blood. The blood of any Burning Saint, or a member of any club affiliated with them, and each of us needs to be on guard at all times, until the threat of the Spiders is eliminated."

"Exactly how long are we supposed to fight the Burning Saints war for them?" Gator asked.

"It's not their war. It's all of ours. If the Spiders take control over Portland, Savannah will be next."

"But we didn't start shit with the Spiders, the Saints did," Gator argued.

"The Spiders are planning on expanding their operation from coast to coast, but they need to take Portland first," Doc explained. "The Saints need more soldiers on the streets, and we need their protection. Without them, we're vulnerable."

"It still feels like we're caught in the middle of some shit we didn't start."

"Sounds like life to me," Doc replied.

"So, what's our next move?" I asked.

"Our next move is to lay low and keep close tabs on our families. I want everyone paired up when you're out, no exceptions. If you see a member of the Spiders, or come across anything out of the ordinary, you report it to me directly."

"That's it?" I snapped.

"What are you looking for, Doom?"

"Oh, I don't know. Maybe a plan for going after the guys that tried to blow up my family."

The words "my family" had never felt so heavy on my lips. My heart was burdened with my love for Lyric and our child and my desire to protect them.

"I know how you feel, Doom," Doc said.

"You have no idea how I feel, and I have no intention of laying low, while the Spiders that tried to take out the people I love are crawling the streets."

I stood and walked out, slamming the door behind me.

* * *

Lyric

The bed dipped and I craned my neck as Doom stretched out beside me. "Hey."

"Hey."

"You look like someone killed your puppy, John Wick."

"Someone tried to kill my woman," he growled.

"Well, there is that." I sighed. "How's Rabbit?"

"He's gonna have some rehab to deal with in the coming months, but he'll be okay."

"Are you sure?"

"Yeah, baby. I promise."

I relaxed and pressed my back against his front, snuggling closer.

He slid his hand across my waist, palming my belly. "I should never have let you go over there."

"Um, hello, you don't *let* me go anywhere. I'm an adult and it's my house. I go where I want to go," I pointed out.

"Lyric, don't get all alpha female on me right now. It wasn't safe, I knew it, and I should have gone with my gut."

"I can't have someone dictate my life, Lin—"

"Jesus Christ, woman, stop. I'm gonna fuckin' dictate it until I know you're safe, hear?"

I sighed. "Okay, honey, I hear you. I know this freaked you out, but I'm okay. You're okay. My house...not so much."

"Dad'll take care of it," he promised. "How's our little blip?"

"He's fine, honey."

"It wasn't Garrett."

"It wasn't?"

"No. Dalton's been working behind the scenes to get him back inside. He was re-arrested two days ago. And this time, his grandma's been indicted on several charges as well, so she's being held without bond. There's been no chatter about her hiring anyone to get to you, but there *is* evidence of another kind. This was a hit from a rival club."

I gasped, rolling to face him. "What kind of rival club?"

"That I can't go into yet."

I stroked his beard. "Baby, how bad is this?"

"It's bad, Angel."

"Am I going to be able to go back to work?"

"Not right away. Need you to work from here for a couple of weeks."

"What about the other women?"

"I'm not responsible for the other women."

I bit my lip. "Well, that's gonna go over well with Liv, I'm sure," I deadpanned.

"Which is why Doc gets paid the big bucks."

"I just don't understand why they'd nuke my house."

"They've been followin' us. They can't touch the compound and they know we come here every week, so they've been bidin' their time. But families should be off-limits."

"You should be off-limits, too, honey," I pointed out.

"If only it were that easy."

"Who's doing this?"

"Not something you need to worry about, Lyric. Put it out of your mind."

Oh, how I loved it when he treated me like the little woman, said me, never.

I rolled my eyes. "Do I have you for the rest of the night? Can we make some food and watch a movie or something? I really need you close."

He kissed me gently. "Yeah, Angel. You got me."

* * *

Two days later, I had information Doom would rather I not have sealed in a manila envelope and hidden behind the sofa in my office.

I'd had Shawn do some digging for me and I now had information that could prove useful, provided I could sneak out of my

155

prison without being detected. For the moment, however, I was starving and I was in the mood for bacon. Probably because I could smell it wafting from the kitchen.

"I did not agree to be locked up for a week, Tristan!" Olivia bellowed as I made my way toward the aroma.

"Don't give a fuck," Doc retorted.

"I'm going to Clementine's, then."

"No you're not."

"Tris—"

"You're stayin' here until the threat's eliminated, Olivia. End of story. You wanna argue more about it, we can do that later. I gotta go."

I heard a feminine screech, then a loud crash and Doc bellowing, "Goddammit, woman!"

I rushed into the room to find a cast iron skillet on the floor, bacon and grease all over the tile, and a huge divot in the wall.

"What the fuck?" Doc demanded.

"I brought the bacon *and* fried it up in the pan," she screeched.

"You could have hit me!" Doc accused.

"Please. I pulled my punch. If I'd wanted to hit you, I would have," Olivia snapped. "You know how good my aim is."

Doc put his hand out. "Lyric, don't move. You might slip on the grease."

"Well, that was a waste of perfectly good bacon," I pointed out, but stayed where I was. The last thing I needed was another broken leg.

"Don't encourage her," Doc growled.

"I want out of this fucking barn, Tristan," Olivia seethed.

Doc shook his head. "One week, Liv."

"Go, Doc," I said. "We'll clean this up."

He scowled at Liv, but still managed to kiss her quickly, then walked out the door.

"Fucking pain in my ass," she hissed as she started to clean up the mess.

"At the risk of being nosy, do you think you might be a little hard on Doc?" I asked.

She shook her head. "Some days I feel like I'm in quicksand, you know? I have no idea what the fuck that man wants from me. We aren't even a couple. We fuck occasionally, we have no deep feelings for one another, but he insists on whisking me away whenever there's some kind of threat."

I was pretty sure the fact they didn't have deep feelings for one another was a lie, but I wasn't going to say that out loud... she was still holding the skillet.

"Can you get us out of here?" I asked, switching subjects.

"What do you mean?"

"Secretly. Can you find a way to get us out of here clandestinely?"

She dumped the skillet in the sink and faced me. "Why?"

"Not here."

She smiled slowly, evilly, and cocked her head. "Well, well, Lyric Morgan, what did you have in mind?"

We cleaned up the grease and headed to my office.

* * *

It took two days to put our plan into motion and by the time we got Doc, Doom, and Alamo out of the compound, we were both nervous wrecks. Me more than Olivia. I got the impression Olivia was a pro at subterfuge...me, not so much. Jasmine was at her salon with her best friend, Parker, under heavy guard. Dash and Badger were out on a run for one of the bars the club owned, and Quin and Willow were being watched by Gator and Milky here at the compound.

Olivia and I were technically being watched as well, however, our girls were going to distract them with questions about the war or something Gator and Milky would argue over, so that we could skedaddle and head to our rendezvous spot as soon as feasibly possible.

"Jazz is ready," Olivia said.

"Good."

"Did you turn off your phone?" Olivia whispered.

"Not yet," I said. "If Doom sees it's off, he'll investigate why. I'll wait until we're on the road."

"He's going to freak the fuck out."

"He won't if this works."

"Even if it works, he's going to freak the fuck out."

I sighed. She was right. He would. But the end was going to justify the means for me, and right now, that's all that mattered.

"Eagle one to Iron Mountain, the coast is clear," Willow whispered.

"Who the fuck are you calling a mountain?" Olivia ground out.

"Well, you're tall and you're fierce, ergo…mountain."

"Jesus, you're weird," Olivia said. "Cute and I love the hell out of you, but you're fucking weird."

Willow grinned and handed me her keys. "Go before Gator figures out you're gone."

We headed out to Willow's car which was parked around the corner, and drove into downtown Savannah. Jasmine was getting ready for a soft launch of a new salon and was using the space as a ruse for our plan, so we parked in the back where we wouldn't be seen from the road.

Turning off the car, I faced Olivia. "Ready?"

"Born ready."

I nodded, grabbed my bag, and we headed inside. Jasmine was waiting and raised her finger to her lips before leading us to the back where the treatment rooms were. She'd obviously managed to ditch her 'detail.'

"Parker's ready when you are," she whispered.

"Do it," I instructed.

Like a well-choreographed routine, I heard two feminine screams, a few crashes, then some rather creative cursing before Tammy, old lady to Sugar Bear, Savannah Chapter President of the Spiders was walked out, fully naked, with her hands zip-tied behind her back, closely followed by Lulu, wearing only panties and a look of total confusion. Olivia had a strong hold on Tammy, while Parker gripped Lulu.

"Goddammit," Tammy snapped. "I knew all this was too good to be true."

"What?" Lulu said.

"That's Lyric. Doom's woman." Tammy nodded to Jasmine. "And that's Alamo's bitch. Fuck, I shoulda known. The freebies were a trick to get us here."

Jasmine smiled. "Yeah. Sorry, not sorry."

"Right. Well, I wasn't expecting you to be so, um, naked. Can we get them some robes?" I asked Jasmine.

"I'm not ashamed of my body," Tammy declared. "Are you sayin' I should be ashamed of my body?"

"No, not at all," I rushed to say.

Crap, this was not going well. I needed to get the upper hand back.

"She's been doing that polenta stuff," Lulu said.

"Pilates," Tammy corrected.

"Well, you look great," I said, diverting my eyes.

"What do you want, bitch?" Tammy snapped.

"I was hoping we could make peace."

"Why the fuck would we make peace with you?"

"To be nice?" I asked, hopefully.

Tammy let out an inelegant snort. "Make your demand, bitch, so we can get the fuck outta here. Our men are gonna love this." She leaned forward. "Specifically, making each one of you pay. Slowly."

"Look, there must be some common ground here," I said. "You've got kids—"

"You leave my kids out of this."

"I'd love to leave your kids out of this, Tammy, but the drone that dropped the pipe bomb on my house didn't give me the same consideration."

That got her attention, so I pressed on.

"Your man's club dropped a bomb on my house. On. My. House. It landed inches from the nursery. *Inches*, Tammy. Inches from where my child is going to sleep." I laid my hand on my still flat belly. "And if I'd been standing by the window, it could have killed me and my unborn child. Are you alright with that? If my man did that to one of you, would you be okay with it? We have to figure out a way to make our men stop the war."

She squared her shoulders but didn't look at me.

"We are level-headed, smart women. There is no reason why we can't come to some kind of agreement that will be beneficial to all of us."

"Sugar don't take orders from no woman," Lulu pointed out.

"Shut up, Lu," Tammy snapped.

"Look, maybe we can't get them to stop fighting amongst themselves, but we have the power of the pussy," Olivia pointed out. "We have some influence."

"Exactly," I said. "Can we agree to keep the fighting on neutral ground, because, I swear to god, if someone comes after my home again, I'm going to lose my religion."

"And what's in it for us if we agree to this Geneva Cuntvention?" Tammy demanded.

"The peace of mind that our kids can walk to the bus stop without being killed by a pipe bomb?" I said.

Tammy smirked. "I don't worry about that shit."

"I know," I said. "Because our men don't go around bombing innocent people!"

Tammy shrugged and I seriously wanted to smack her skanky face.

"Your little brother's name is Joseph Fines, right?"

She glared at me.

"And he's in county awaiting trial, right?" I asked.

"What about it?"

"He pulled Stein as his public defender, correct?"

Tammy's face paled and I knew I'd hit a nerve. "Yeah."

"I take it the Spiders aren't getting involved? Otherwise, why would they leave him to the fates of a public defender. Especially one with such a low win rate."

She scowled.

"Right. Here's the deal. You get your men to back the fuck off, and I'll represent him."

My girls gasped and Jasmine even tried to argue, but I held my hand up and shook my head.

"I want peace, Jazz."

"At what cost?" she challenged. "Our men aren't going to accept you representing a Spider."

"Is your brother a Spider, Tammy?"

She shook her head.

"He's not a Spider, Jazz. Problem solved."

"Jesus Christ, chickie, balls of steel," Olivia said.

"Do you agree, Tammy?" I pressed.

160

Tammy scowled at me for several tense seconds before nodding.

"Untie them," I said, and Parker and Olivia released them.

They dressed and scurried out of the salon and I slid down the wall onto the floor and dropped my head to my knees.

What the hell did I just do?

NINETEEN

Lyric

"UM, LIV, LYRIC, you need to get back to the compound," Jasmine said, waving her phone in the air. "Willow said Doom and Doc are on their way back and they're pissed."

"What are the odds we'll beat them back?" I asked.

"Unlikely," Olivia said. "Come on. I'll drive."

I followed her toward the foyer and just as we hit the doors, Alamo came barreling in.

"Are you *fuckin'* kidding me?" he growled. "Jesus Christ." He pulled his phone out and put it to his ear. "Doc, they're here.

Yeah. Yeah. No problem." He slid his phone back in his pocket and glared at us. "Back inside."

I slid my bag over my shoulder. "We should—"

"Get the fuck back inside," Alamo demanded.

About ten minutes later, the roar of Harley pipes rumbled outside and my stomach churned as my fate drew closer. I had no idea how much, if anything, I was going to tell Doom tonight. I knew I'd have to tell him something eventually, but right now, I just wanted to curl up beside him and have him hold me.

Unfortunately, I'd put myself in a potentially dangerous situation, so I was pretty sure snuggling and soothing words of comfort weren't going to be on the table for me.

Doom walked in, followed closely by Doc, and stepped over to me. His eyes studied me before taking my bag off my shoulder, handing me a helmet, and gently grabbing my arm without a word and tugging me outside. He shoved everything into the saddlebag and faced me.

"Put your helmet on."

"Are we going—?"

"Put your goddamn helmet on before I fuckin' lose my shit, Lyric."

I put my helmet on, then climbed on behind him and we headed back to the compound. Once inside the safety of the gates, Doom walked me upstairs and into our room, dropped my bag on the bed, then turned and left me again.

Without a word.

Booger had glared at me from his cat tower but decided not to get involved. Smart cat.

I took a minute to freshen up, then decided to go downstairs for something to eat. Only to find I couldn't open the door. I jiggled the handle and it wouldn't budge. I thought it was stuck, but when I bent down to peer in the old-fashioned lock, I realized the key was gone. Doom had taken the key. I was locked in.

"Are you kidding me?"

I banged on the door.

"Doom!" I called, and banged again.

Pulling my phone out of my bag, I powered it up and called him. He didn't answer. No surprise there, so when his voicemail beeped, I said, *"Lincoln, I'd highly suggest you get your ass up here and unlock this door, or I'm going to a hotel and we are done."*

Once I hung up, I called Willow. "Hey."

"I'm locked in."

"You are?"

"Yes. Can you come let me out?"

"I'm not there," she said. "I'm sorry. I'm at home."

"How did you manage that?"

"Honestly, I don't know. Gator, Mouse, and Milky are here with us. Dash is there, though. I think there's an all-hands."

"Us?"

"Jasmine and Parker."

"He made it so no one was here to free me," I seethed.

"Sounds like it," Willow agreed.

"I'm going to kill him."

"There's always Olivia. She's not here," Willow said. "I have no idea where she is."

I sighed. "Probably locked in Doc's room."

"Maybe."

"What about Quin?" I asked.

"I don't know. I haven't seen her all day," she said. "I'm sorry, honey. If I thought we had a chance of getting out of here without being seen, I'd totally make a break for it. Gator's watching me extra close."

"It's okay," I said. "I'll figure something out."

"Good luck."

"Thanks."

I hung up and called Quin.

"Hey, Lyric."

"Are you here?" I asked. "At the compound?"

"Yes, why?"

"Because Doom locked me in our room."

"Shut up, really?"

I paced the room. "Yes, and I need someone to come and let me out or I'm going to murder him in his sleep."

"Well, if I had the key, I'd totally come up there and free you, but I don't."

"Shit," I hissed.

"I can storm into the meeting and demand he give it to me, though," she offered.

"No, that's okay. But will you help me hide his body in the morning?"

"Absolutely. Just let me know where and when."

"Thanks."

I hung up and dropped my phone on the nightstand. I was emotionally drained and exhausted, so I decided to lie down for a minute.

What I didn't expect was to wake up in the dark with my man sitting in the chair by the window staring at me like some weird ass crazy person.

"Fifty-two minutes," he said, and I sat up.

"What?"

Booger awoke beside me, stretching before moving to his cat tower and falling back to sleep. So much for a united front.

"I didn't know where you were for fifty-two minutes," Doom continued. "Technically, you weren't where you were supposed to be for a fuck of a lot longer than that, but I 'lost' you for fifty-two minutes."

"I was fine."

He cocked his head. "Were you fine, Lyric?"

"Yes."

"Or were you alone in a building with the old ladies of two of the most dangerous bikers in Savannah?" he bellowed.

"Who told you?"

"No one fuckin' told me. Alamo pulled the surveillance tapes. And this brings up the second problem. No one fuckin' told me," he bellowed.

I relaxed a little. My girls kept the code. This was good.

"Lyric. Why the fuck were you in the salon with Tammy and Lulu?"

"We were making a peace treaty."

He dragged his hands down his face. "Are you fuckin' kiddin' me?"

"I'd never kid about a peace treaty."

"Jesus Fucking Christ woman, I'm holding on by a thread

here, do not make light of any of this."

"You locked me in our room as though I'm your chattel, so how about you start by apologizing, Lincoln? Then, maybe we can have an adult conversation about what happened today, instead of you just sitting there pounding your chest like some Neanderthal, demanding answers and giving me orders!"

"I locked you in so I'd know where you were because you have a tendency to fuckin' *disappear*." He yelled, "disappear," and I scowled.

"Okay, well, if you're not going to apologize, I'd like you to leave."

"I'm not leavin', Lyric." He rose to his feet and started to undress, heading to the bathroom. He managed to get his T-shirt off.

"Better grab a blanket, then. You're not sleeping here."

Doom stalked back to the bed, reaching for me, gently grabbing my legs, and tugging me down the mattress. I let out a quiet squeal as he leaned over me and cupped my chin. "Let's get something straight right now. It doesn't matter how pissed we are at one another, we sleep together. I don't believe in the old adage don't go to bed mad, because sometimes you just need to sleep in order to get a clear head, but you and I'll never sleep apart. Understand?"

I wrinkled my nose, because I didn't really want to sleep with him. I mean, I did. But not until he apologized and groveled a little.

Although, I *could* accidentally push him out of bed—

"Lyric?"

"It's your funeral," I grumbled.

"Did you eat?"

"Hello? Locked in our room?" I snapped.

"Baby, I left you a sandwich in the fridge."

"*Baby*, I'm growing our baby in my belly, so I've been asleep. I didn't know you left me a sandwich in the fridge."

He switched the nightstand lamp on, stalked to the mini fridge, and pulled out the sandwich he'd obviously put there while I was asleep. He also handed me a Sprite.

I sat up against the headboard and took a bite of the sandwich and swallowed. "Are you going to apologize now?"

"Why the fuck would you take it upon yourself to start a war with the Spiders' old ladies?"

"Apparently not."

"Lyric."

I huffed. "We weren't trying to start a war. We were trying to end a war that you men just seem to keep escalating."

"What makes you think these women are any less dangerous than their old men? They're seasoned criminals as much as the bikers they ride with."

I shrugged. "Well, someone had to do something."

"Did you ever stop to think that while you were busy assembling your little mock UN, you could have just as easily started a cat fight in the middle of our dog fight?"

"But we didn't." I glanced around the room. "As you can see, I'm here, perfectly safe, as are the rest of the women."

"That's not the point. I didn't know where you were and could only assume the worst. And what makes the whole thing unbearable is that you were actually in a dangerous place. It makes my blood boil that you would even put yourself and the baby in harm's way like that."

I sighed. "I'm sorry that I worried you, but Tammy and I came up with a deal, so all you have to do is worry about the club. Families are off-limits."

Doom cocked his head. "Do I want to know?"

"She has to come through first, so maybe let's wait and see if that happens."

"Woman, what have you done?"

"I told her that if she convinced her man to get the heat off of us, meaning women and kids, and my fucking house, I'd represent her brother, who's currently sitting in county awaiting trial."

"Jesus fucking Christ!" he bellowed, stalking out the door, and slamming it behind him.

"That went well," I told Booger, who was peeking out from his cat tower.

"Meow."

"Thanks for having my back, Booger. I appreciate it."

"Meow."

I finished my food and cleaned up, then made my way downstairs to look for Doom. Lucky for him, our door was now unlocked. I found him in Doc's office, and I was granted access, greeted by two very angry looking bikers.

"I'm gonna come back," I said, pointing to the exit.

"You're gonna sit your ass down," Doom growled.

"Uh, no, I'm not," I countered. "I won't be spoken to that way, and you well know it."

"Lyric, wait," Doc said. "Will you please explain this deal you made with Tammy?"

"Why, yes, Doc, I'd be happy to," I said, and stepped further inside, scowling up at Doom. "That's how polite people get information, Lincoln, in case you want to take notes."

He dragged his hands down his face and paced the room.

"It's pretty straight forward, Doc. I told Tammy I didn't want anyone touching my house again, and I felt kids and wives should be off-limits and she should figure out a way to make that happen. If she did, I told her I'd represent her brother. Honestly, he's gotten a raw deal. He's young and I think he's being railroaded. It'll be an open and shut case, but the public defender he pulled is kind of an idiot, so he'll lose and Tammy knows it."

Doc crossed his arms. "It's an interesting tack to take, Lyric, but I'd rather you not have done that without clearing it with Doom first. You don't know what you're dealing with here, especially with Tammy. She's bad news and I'd appreciate it if you didn't have any further contact with her."

"Well, I can't do that, considering I might be representing her brother."

I heard Doom growl deep in his throat but he didn't form words or sentences.

"As much as I wish we could," Doc said with a sigh, "we can't put the genie back in the bottle, but you cannot meet with her alone, Lyric. If Tammy manages to make some kind of deal with her old man, and they guarantee no more hits on families, then, yes, you represent her brother, and we'll have your back. But I need to know you won't meet with her alone. Ever."

I glanced at Doom who looked like his head might explode.

"I can do that," I promised.

"Thanks, babe," Doc said. "I'm gonna let you two... ah... talk. We can deal with anything that comes up tomorrow. Try and get some rest."

"Is Olivia okay?" I asked.

"She's fine."

"Where is she?" I asked.

"Upstairs."

"In your room?"

"Yes."

"*Locked* in your room?" I pressed.

He smirked. "No."

I glared at Doom. "Okay, I'll see you in the morning."

I made my way upstairs and into the bathroom. I debated locking the door before Doom could follow me inside, but I figured he'd just break it down, so I decided against it. I stripped down to my T-shirt and panties and brushed my teeth, pulling my hair into a ponytail and then took my anti-nausea pill.

When I came out, Doom was back in the chair, his head in his hands, looking like the weight of the world was on his shoulders again.

"Do you not trust me?" he asked.

"What do you mean?"

"It's a pretty straightforward question, Lyric." He met my eyes. "Do you not trust me?"

"None of this has anything to do with trust."

"Baby, I'm trying to keep you safe and you're fightin' me at every turn."

I sighed, making my way to him and sitting in his lap, straddling his hips. "I get it now."

"Yeah?"

"Yeah." I stroked his beard. "We're running into a battle of the alphas."

"Is that what we're doing?"

"I've been on my own for a long time, honey," I said. "I have never had anyone 'do' for me. I'm the head of my family, so to speak. I essentially raised my sisters, and still raise Melody to a certain extent, so when I see an issue, I take care of it. I have resources, so I used those resources to get information on Tammy and I just went with it. Maybe it wasn't the wisest thing to do, and perhaps I could have given you the information instead and had you deal with it, but can we please acknowledge that it was a good plan and it all worked out?"

"But it could have gone to shit."

"Yes, you're right, it could have. And that's bad on my part. I promise, I'll be more careful in the future. But it was a fucking good plan," I prompted. "Right?"

He sighed. "Yeah, baby, it was. I wouldn't have handled it the same way, but it was a good plan."

"And...?"

"And I'm sorry I locked you in..." He paused and shook his head. "No, actually, I'm not. If you pull something like that again, Lyric, I'm gonna fuckin' handcuff you to the bed."

"You have handcuffs?"

"I do."

I pressed my pussy against his already rock hard cock. "Maybe we can play."

He shook his head pulling my T-shirt over my head. "No. There will never be a time I want you restrained in bed. I like your hands on me."

Cupping my breasts, he drew one nipple, then the other into his mouth. I dropped my head back as he lavished attention on my breasts, sucking, biting and rolling my nipples into tight beads.

Pulling my head down, he kissed me, then stood, lifting me off of him and setting me on my feet. Divesting us both of the rest of our clothing, he guided me to the bed and gripped my chin. "On your knees."

I nodded and climbed onto the mattress, scrambling onto all fours, my pussy contracting with need, and I knew I was already soaked. The bed dipped as he knelt behind me and I bit my lip in anticipation, but when the slap to my ass came, I wasn't prepared for the near orgasm it produced.

"One day, Angel, you're gonna learn to obey me." Slap. "Until then, I'm gonna need to teach you a few lessons." Another slap.

I certainly planned to never obey, because these kinds of lessons were delicious.

He slid into me and I pressed back against him to take him deeper. He pulled out of me and I whimpered as he slid his finger inside of me, wanting his dick, but then he pushed back inside of me, pushing his slick digit into my very tight hole and I gasped at the intrusion.

"You okay?" he asked.

"Hell, yeah," I said. "Harder, Doom."

He obliged.

He slammed into me, harder and harder, his finger fucking my ass in rhythm with his dick and I came so hard and fast, I fell to the mattress, screaming his name, my body shaking as my pussy contracted around his cock.

His hand connected with my ass before my orgasm was finished, and he growled, "On your knees, Lyric."

I got on my knees, where he promptly came on my ass, sliding his fingers through the wetness, then pressing inside of me again.

"Do *not* move," he ordered.

My arms were shaking with the effort, but I did not move, and he slid two fingers into my pussy, and his thumb into my ass, pumping until I thought for sure I'd lose my mind. Then his dick was inside of me again and his hand connected with my ass and I screamed his name.

"Get there, baby," I begged.

He buried himself deep again, then squeezed my tender bottom and rasped, "Now, Angel."

I came, falling to the bed as my orgasm washed over me. Doom caught me and guided me to his chest, spooning with me and holding me close.

"Jesus, you scared the shit out of me today," he whispered. "Don't ever fuckin' do that again."

"I can't make that promise, honey." Smiling, I reached behind me to grab his thigh. "But I *will* do better about telling you my plans."

"Stay put," he said, and pulled out of me, heading to the bathroom and returning with a wet washcloth to clean me up.

I rolled to face him as he climbed back into bed with me.

"So…"

"Yeah?"

"I like anal."

He dropped his head back and laughed. "Yeah, I picked up on that."

"I also like being spanked."

"Picked up on that as well."

"Which means, I may just disobey you on the regular," I warned, running my finger over his Dogs tattoo.

He frowned. "That wasn't the outcome I intended."

"Liar."

Doom chuckled, kissing me gently. "Love you, Angel."

I stroked his cheek. "Love you too, honey."

TWENTY

Lyric

TWO DAYS LATER, Doom called me into Doc's office and I felt like I was being summoned to detention.

As I walked in, Doom closed the door behind me, and Doc waved to the chair across from his desk. "Everything okay?" I asked.

"Got a message from Sugar Bear," Doc said.

My heart raced. "Do I want to know?"

"Families are off-limits," he said, taking his seat.

I gasped. "Really?"

"Yeah," he said. "But only here in Savannah. Sugar won't guarantee outside chapters. He also won't admit to anyone this is happenin'. It's an unwritten law, but he's made it clear to anyone within a hundred mile radius. Families are safe."

"That's great." I glanced at Doom, his face like stone. "It's

173

great, right?"

"Don't trust the fucker," he admitted.

"Well, we have to start somewhere," I said. "I think this is encouraging. And now, Tammy's brother has a chance to make a good life for himself."

"If you can get him out," Doc said.

"Oh, I can get him out. That kid's about as innocent as my mom claims to have been on her wedding night."

"I'm still puttin' sensors on your house to warn us about incoming drones and shit," Doom said.

"That's fine," I said. "Do whatever you need to do. Put sharpshooters up there. Just make it quick. I want to go home, honey."

Doom nodded and I stood, wrapping my arms around him with a grin. "Can we all just acknowledge what an incredible badass I am now?"

Doc chuckled. "I don't know that it's a good idea for me to feed the beast, Lyric."

"Well, I'll take that as your acknowledgement." I grinned up at Doom. "And you. You're going to take me shopping for house stuff to make up for doubting me."

"I never doubted you."

"You doubted me."

He rolled his eyes. "Let's go shopping, brat."

After grabbing a list and my purse, he took me shopping.

* * *

Lyric

Four months later...

It was move in day. Finally. Sterling had worked overtime to get the house put back together, better than ever, and I'd even had the chance to redesign the kitchen, which I'd always wanted to do. It looked far more 'period' than it had before because I'd hidden all of the appliances behind antique cabinets and furniture. It was magnificent.

After much discussion with Doom and his dad, we'd decided

to turn the basement into a fully functional apartment for Sterling if there ever came a time when he shouldn't live by himself. Being the alpha male he was, because the apple didn't fall far from the tree, he'd done a lot of growling and arguing, but in the end, he'd compromised and said he'd do it only if he could put a urinal in the bathroom. I'd shuddered, but agreed to it, provided it was hidden in a small alcove.

In the meantime, the apartment could be used by Melody or Harmony when they came to visit and would afford them a little more privacy. It was something I should have done sooner, but just didn't think of it.

Doom and I were officially 'hitched.' It had been a small ceremony in my back yard with the club and my family, but it was perfect. We'd both signed prenups, but let's be honest, divorce wasn't an option. Just murder.

Things with the Spiders weren't good, but as promised, the conflict was staying away from the women and kids. Doom didn't share what was going on with the clubs and I didn't ask. I didn't really want to know and I figured if I needed to know, he'd tell me.

In the end, Joey's trial never happened. Shawn had uncovered evidence to prove Joey's innocence, so the case was thrown out and Joey was released from jail. Tammy was ecstatic. I warned the kid about hanging out with the wrong crowd, but I knew he'd never listen. He was trapped in the Spiders' web and there'd never be an easy way out for him.

"Directing," Doom reminded me as we walked into the house.

"Yeah, honey, I know."

"In a chair."

"Yep."

"If you try to lift a lamp, I'm gonna lose my shit," he warned.

"So, there'll be spanking?" I asked hopefully.

He rolled his eyes. "There will be if you sit in that chair and direct."

I smiled big. "Deal."

Doom guided me to my snuggle chair, now in the front

room, and kissed me quickly before heading back outside to start moving the rest of our stuff in.

For the next hour, the club moved all of my newly purchased furniture in, including office furniture, basement furniture, and the baby's set up. Once they were done, they left us alone with the plan to return the U-haul and come back later for the housewarming party that the ladies had planned on our behalf.

"Ready to see the nursery?" Doom asked, walking into the front room.

I clapped my hands. "Yes."

I reached out to him and he took my hands, hoisting me out of the seat, and positioning himself behind me. I waddled up the stairs with him supporting me from behind and I teared up as we made our way down the hallway. All of the family photos we'd spent hours sorting through had been framed and hung on both sides of the walls, including a couple of gorgeous pictures of Jennifer and Ezra. "When did you hang the pictures?"

"Yesterday," he said.

I faced him. "Were you okay?"

He smiled, stroking my cheek. "Yeah, baby. I was okay. I didn't know why you wanted them on the wall, but I see it now."

I nodded. "They're part of our family. Even if they're not here physically, they're part of our hearts."

He nodded. "Yeah." He kissed me gently. "Thank you."

"You're welcome."

Doom turned me back around and guided me into the nursery and I gasped. "Oh, honey, it's perfect."

The club had transformed the room into the cutest little biker's bedroom anyone could imagine. Our ultrasound had revealed a very big boy, so we were ecstatic to plan for the next generation of bikers. A black crib sat against the wall with a painting of a vintage Harley-Davidson hanging above it.

The changing table was fully stocked with diapers, wipes, powder, and cream, and they'd anchored the dresser to the wall so it wouldn't fall. There was a glider in the corner with a baby leather cut, complete with Dogs logo on the back, all ready for the baby's patch to be attached, and I just couldn't contain my gratitude.

Wrapping my arms around my man, I burst into tears and hugged him tight. "Thank you. I love it. It's perfect."

He chuckled, stroking my back. "You're welcome."

As we stood in the middle of our child's bedroom, I sent up a silent prayer of thanks for the miracles that had been lavished on me. I don't know what I did to deserve them, but I would never take them for granted.

EPILOGUE

Lyric

Two months later…

"**D**OOM," I MOANED, coming awake as pain sliced through my belly. I reached for his arm and squeezed. Hard. "Lincoln."

He knifed up. "I'm awake. What's wrong?"

"He's coming."

"He's early."

"I'll let you have a conversation with your son when he's old enough to understand words. For the moment, however, we should probably get to the hospit—aaah…" More pain radiated and I couldn't breathe.

Doom slid off the mattress and turned on his lamp, then made his way to my side of the bed. "Okay, baby, you got this. Take some deep breaths. I'm going to get your bag and we'll head out."

"Okay," I whispered.

Doom helped me sit up, and I gripped the edge of the bed as I attempted to do my breathing exercises.

"It's not helping!" I growled.

"I know, Angel," Doom commiserated, as he kneeled in front of me. "Lift."

I lifted my feet and he helped me slide my feet into a pair of maternity sweatpants, then pulled them up my body. After zipping me into my hoodie, he lifted me off the bed and wrapped an arm around my waist. "Okay, baby, let's get you in the car."

We moved slowly down the stairs and into the garage where he gingerly loaded me into the Volvo and buckled me in. We stopped twice to wait out contractions and then I had another one while he was securing my seatbelt, so just getting ready to go took forever, but once Doom was finally in the driver seat, we headed out and I tried my best not to scream every time the pain made me feel like I might die.

Doom took my hand and gave it a gentle squeeze. "You got this, Angel."

"No, I don't actually think I do."

Pulling up to the hospital, Doom helped me inside and a nurse was waiting with a wheelchair. "We'll get you settled into a room, then you can fill out the paperwork," she offered.

"What about the bag?" I asked.

"I'll get it when you're comfortable," Doom said.

For the next two hours, I was subjected to poking, prodding, and the torturous 'checking,' until it was determined I could have an epidural.

"Once the doc gives you the epidural, we can break your water," the nurse informed me.

This was all great information, however, it ended up taking a little longer than expected, so by the time the doctor arrived to administer the epidural, I was about to kill someone. And that someone was Doom because he was the closest to me.

"Okay, Lyric," Dr. Morther said gently, "I'm going to have you bend over like a cat and I need you not to move. It's easier than it sounds, but it's important."

I nodded and Doom helped me swing my legs over the side of the hospital bed, taking my hands and holding me as I dropped my head to his shoulder. Dr. Morther slid the needle into my back and all of a sudden the pain of my contractions stopped and I let out a sigh of relief.

I met Doom's eyes and stroked his cheek. "I'm so sorry I've been a shrew."

He chuckled. "You're not a shrew, Angel. You're in pain. Don't even give it another thought."

A nurse and Dr. Morther helped position me back into the bed so I could keep the epidural in place, and then I was given space to sleep since nothing was really happening yet.

"Doc and Olivia are here," Doom said. "So are Alamo and Jasmine."

"Oh, honey, Olivia doesn't need to be here. This must be killing her."

"Let our friend decide what she can handle," Doom suggested. "You focus on having our baby."

I grabbed his hand. "Tell Doc to let her off the hook."

"Okay, baby. I'll take care of it." He leaned down and kissed me. "*If* you rest."

I closed my eyes and nodded.

* * *

Doom

Lyric fell asleep almost immediately and I used the reprieve to step outside. I still hadn't grabbed her bag from the car and I knew she'd need a few things once the baby came.

"How is she?" Willow asked as soon as I stepped into the hallway. Dash, Badger, and Quin smiled in anticipation as I walked out.

"Asleep for the moment," I said.

I saw Olivia pull away from Doc, wiping her tears and forcing a smile. "Do you need anything?"

Jesus, this woman was made of steel. "I was just going to grab Lyric's bag from the car."

"I can do that," Olivia offered.

"Are you sure?"

"Yeah. It'll give me something to do. Got the keys?"

I nodded and handed them to her. "It's parked in B7."

"Okay."

"Thanks, sweetheart."

"No problem."

"I'll come with you," Willow said, and the women headed to the elevators.

"Lyric's worried about Liv," I told Doc.

He nodded. "She wants to be here. I told her she didn't have to be, but she was adamant."

"Well, let her know if she needs to bail, Lyric understands."

"Thanks, brother."

"I'm gonna go back in."

Doc smiled. "Good luck."

I'd been back in the room for just a few minutes when the nurse walked in and discovered Lyric's water had broken on its own, which meant we were close, and the doctor walked in soon after, checking her to declare she was dilated to ten and fully effaced, so it was time to push.

"We're going to back the epidural off just a little so you can feel enough to push," the doctor said. "Ready?"

"No," Lyric retorted, and I smiled.

"You got this, Angel."

Thirty minutes later, Sterling Ezra Marxx came screaming into the world. Nine pounds six ounces, twenty-three inches long, a full head of dark hair, and he was my healing.

Lyric kissed his forehead as she sobbed and held him close. "Hey, beautiful boy. Oh my word, you look just like your daddy." She smiled up at me. "He's perfect."

I smiled through my own watery eyes and stroked her cheek, kissing her gently, then our son. "He is. So are you. Thank you, Angel. For everything."

My rage was quieted, my demons were gone, and I'd finally found peace.

I'd been given a second chance at love and I was going to cherish it forever.

.

ABOUT PIPER

Piper Davenport writes from a place of passion and intrigue, combining elements of romance and suspense with strong modern-day heroes and heroines.

She currently resides in pseudonymia under the dutiful watch of the Writers Protection Agency.

Like Piper's FB page and get to know her!
(www.facebook.com/piperdavenport)

Twitter: @piper_davenport

Made in the USA
Coppell, TX
14 February 2023

12808370R10107